MW01613450

Slippery When Wet

A Collection of Australian short stories

EDITION 2

Published by Australian Roadside Services Pty Ltd.
Printed by PostScript Printing

Slippery When Wet Competition ~ First published 2002.
Copyright © 2003.
Edition 2 first published 2003.
Reprinted 2007.

CONTENTS

FOREWORD

David Larkin
Director, Australian Roadside Services
Sponsors of the Slippery When Wet Short Story Competition.

Australian Roadside Services has the pleasure of sponsoring the 2003 annual Slippery When Wet Short Story Competition from which winning and finalist entries are published in this short story compilation. We envisage Slippery When Wet as a vehicle for Australian writers of all ages to unleash their imaginations and share their tales of the road; this being the only criteria for entry. Slippery When Wet entries are judged on plot, characterisation and relevance to theme, with a particular emphasis on the story's originality.

Road transport has continued to play a major part in Australia's economy. Our contact with the industry makes us aware of the range of characters and experiences that one may encounter when traveling the roads. We hope that Slippery When Wet will continue to unravel the many roadside adventures lived and dreamt by our authors, for years to come.

In partnership with the Eastern Writers' Group of Victoria, whose talented members have formed the Slippery When Wet judging panel and has provided guidance throughout Slippery When Wet's journey, we are proud to introduce the following winning stories, which precede the stories of our Slippery When Wet finalists:

FIRST PRIZE: *Entangled* by Amanda le Bas de Plumerot.

SECOND PRIZE: *Cruise Control* by John Holton.

THIRD PRIZE: *Shell Past Ajar* by Stella Prideaux.

I would also like to thank the Eastern Writers' Group for the fantastic stories contributed by its members; *Stock Part No.* by James Vanselow, *Just Us* by Vicki Thornton , *Knight of the Road* by Judy Buckingham and *While He's Driving* by Liliane Grace.

The Slippery When Wet Anthology contains boundless adventures kindled by the imagination and inspired by great travels across our vast continent. A plethora of tales with twists, tragedy, fantasy and classic Aussie humour; Slippery When Wet is a portal to the colourful experiences that our country's roads have to offer, journeys of self exploration we come to experience throughout our travels and the bizarre characters that present themselves along the way. Sit back, free your imagination and enjoy for the ride that awaits you between the following pages!

David Larkin

ENTANGLED

By Amanda le Bas de Plumenot

When she was a girl she would imagine her wedding. It was of course in the biggest church, with carillon pealing. Warm spring air carried the sound of birdsong down the aisle with her, stray petals from apple and peach blossom swirled at her feet. She could see the creamy lace bodice of her dress shimmering with clusters of freshwater pearls, the skirts belling about her in a satin cloud like one of those double fuchsia flowers, her feet, pointed and elegant as a ballerina's. On her head the veil – a drift of lace light as a spider's web. She'd be holding a cluster of gardenias with tendrils of jasmine curling about. She would waft down the aisle like a fragrant drift of silvery mist.

Her dad was always there, in the picture. He was by her side, trussed like a penguin. She saw him so perfect with his shoulders straight and square, his cheeks shaved clean. Through the shimmer of veil she would see his Adam's apple resting on his bowtie, catch the glow of his gardenia reflected in the shine of his shoes, smell the musk of his aftershave. He would smile and swell with pride and look to her mum, sitting in the front pew, dabbing her eyes with a lace hanky. In the dream the church was filled with people and she looked across the smiling faces of friends and relatives as she passed them by, gliding on a path of petals.

Trouble was, Tom never fitted the dream. She could never even get his name right, he was never anything but "Tom". Even within the depths of the fantasy she couldn't hear him say "I, Thomas James..." When she tried to put him there, standing by the altar, he was always dressed in dirty jeans and a shirt with the arms ripped out. She would see that mullet head turn and those black-Irish eyes look at her. He would smile, a crooked grin through a smear of beard and reach for her with his greasy, filthy hands, not caring about the dress.

Her actual wedding sucked. It was a civil ceremony that she didn't even plan. Tom sprung it on her as a surprise. The witnesses were a couple of blokes he'd met at the pub. She wore an old blue cotton dress with sweat rings under the arms and he wore shorts and a new T-shirt with "shit happens" printed on the front. It seemed romantic at the time. He promised to love her until death. It didn't seem that important at the time, but he never mentioned fidelity in his vows.

So her wedding fantasy was trashed, but she wanted the other good things, a nice house, couple of kids, her friends around her. Nothing exceptional. Nothing huge or expensive, just a normal life. She had that image of being the perfect wife and mother with a hot dinner on the table, kids doing their homework and the breadwinner coming in through the door at around six to kiss her on the cheek. A wild dream of contentment that slipped away like a water shimmer on a hot day. Somehow, they never seemed to be able to save for a deposit on a house and not even their most passionate and abandoned nights of loving could light that essential spark that gets a baby started.

She couldn't say when it was exactly that they decided to give up on the Australian dream. Probably about the time she truly realised that Tom holding down a steady job was as likely as her conceiving a child. Neither was ever going to happen. They sold all their stuff and bought a second-hand campervan.

"Now when someone asks us for our address, we can just say Australia," Tom said. And they drove.

There were always good moments, balanced by the bad. She didn't complain. It's just that this wasn't how she dreamed things would be when she was a girl. She liked the freedom, the lack of responsibility, the lifestyle. She liked living in new places, finding the gifts each new town had to offer. It's just that she was more aware of things with just the two of them together, without a garden and a vacuum cleaner and neighbours to distract her. There isn't that much going on in a campervan. Not like a house. There isn't the option of hiding away in one room and pretending to not notice the other person's errors. Or their absences.

She blamed his parents. Tom. Why would you name your kid after a male cat? Everyone knows what they're like – they go wandering off for days and nights. You don't know if they've been run over or mauled by a dog or taken to the pound or if they're just visiting with some attractive female. The first time it happened she thought he'd been in an accident. She almost went to the police. She'd just got back from her cleaning job and he wasn't home. She asked at the yard where he'd been working. No, he hadn't come to any harm. There were grins and shrugs at the pub. They closed ranks to protect their mate. She cried, angry and helpless, then gave him up.

It looked like he wasn't coming back. She put the campervan in order and started bundling his stuff up for the Salvos. It was all in boxes, ready to go. It didn't amount to much and she'd almost convinced herself she was glad to be rid of him. Then he turned up, four days later, wearing his crooked grin and the same clothes he'd gone off in.

"Where the f**k do you think you've been?"

He just shrugged. "Around." His clothes were clean and he smelt faintly of soap and someone else's perfume. He wore a shadow of stubble. "Come on love," he said. "I'm home, aren't I?" And he slid his arms around her and coaxed her into bed.

They moved on the next day, there was always another town, another caravan park, another job. Another distraction to keep the old tomcat amused. She would sit alone in the van waiting for him to come home. Her guts twisting into acid loops, her head aching. She saw him in every moving shadow, the rhythm of his body being spent on some other woman, his mouth, her red, perfect lips. Some cow from the back paddocks, some bitch in heat. She wonders what the attraction is, what those women have that she doesn't. Perhaps it's just that they have the good sense not to be married to a man like Tom. Deep inside her an old dream dies and a new one is born to take its place.

Now, when she lies in bed, feeling it grow cold, she imagines what it will be like alone. She can fill up the whole bed, chuck out his clothes and own the entire cupboard, spend all the money on things she likes. Stay longer in towns with work she can do and people she gets on with. It pisses her off that he spends money on these women, but she's stopped sharing her money. She keeps it hidden from him. She reads a lot more and she's getting good at crossword puzzles.

He's been gone for nearly a week and she's happy, thinking that in another couple of days she'll go to the supermarket and grab some cartons and pack all his stuff. She's sitting by the campervan with a small fire burning. She likes it when they stay in parks that let them have a fire. She pokes the coals with a stick.

"What do you see when the arrow pierces the flame?" he says. She jumps at the sudden sound of his voice. Her plans crumble like the ashes. He wraps his long arms around her and kisses her forehead, cheek, lips.

"I see that you've been f**king a redhead," She tells him.

He laughs and takes her by the hand. "Come inside with me and I'll show you some f**king."

"Keep your manky dick in your pants, I don't want it. It's probably got some disease on it – AIDS or something. Go disinfect yourself." She lets him lead her inside. He slips his warm hand under her blouse and teases the rigid bud of her nipple. She tells him it was cold sitting by that fire and she reaches for his pants.

"We'll go to the pub," he says later. "Have a nice dinner, hey?"

She washes out of a bucket, puts on clean clothes, brushes her hair, dusts on make up. He watches all this from the bed, then drags on the same slightly grubby clothes he was wearing when he left a week ago. She doesn't want to know where he got the money for a counter meal.

It's bright and warm at the pub and he brings her Bacardi and Coke. She stirs the drink with a red straw, knocking bubbles off the side of the glass so that they drift up and break on the surface.

"What do you see in a swirl of dark rum?" he asks.

"I see you f**king a black woman," She tells him.

He laughs. "You have such sexy imagination."

They leave the next day. It's like he's had enough of this town, or it's had enough of him. Maybe her husband's due back today. Tom doesn't want to meet any husbands.

"We'll go north," he says. "No, west. Orange, maybe, or Alice Springs. I know, Broome. It's beautiful there. We'll go to Broome."

They've got the whole country in front of them. It could take years to get to Broome. She watches the nose of the car as it devours the broken lines of the road. Images of water shimmer in the distance, always fading like dreams as they approach. She sees the black snake of road absorbing hour after hour of their lives until there's nothing left but dried up husks, blowing along in a drift of dust. She hears the drone of the wheels going on forever. Between towns the radio's a static hiss. They are buffeted by passing road-trains that leave them standing in a haze of dirty fumes. They follow trucks for hours and she stares into the faces of condemned animals. There are no gardenias or birdsongs or spring breezes in her life.

He turns his dirty face to her and grins his crooked grin. "What do you see in that sunset at the end of the road there?"

She watches for a long time. Yellow sun and dusty golden-red desert that goes on forever. She stares until the sun is out of sight and her eyes have been burned so she's blinded by negative images. "I see you going down on a blonde with long legs." She feels the cold, hopeless bite of his company. He laughs.

They drive as the light fades and the sky fills with the twisted brilliance of freshwater pearls. When it's finally dark, they stop beside the road. She opens cans and cooks dinner. He makes a cup of tea. They switch on the radio and try to get the ABC but can't be bothered fighting the static. He pulls out a deck of cards and they play. In the corner by the window a spider's made a web.

"What do you see in the tangled threads and eight long limbs?" he asks.

"You and me entwined," She tells him.

She watches the spider huddled in its corner. The web drapes like lace decorated with the bound bodies of its prey. It's drawn them in, roping them with strands of silver grey and hanging them like seed pearls in a dusty veil. The spider watches her, it's body black matt, hunched in the corner. It tests the web, extending two legs that lie like oil marks against the pale sheen of silk.

Tom sees her watching it. "Scared of it, are ya? Scared it might bite? Here, I'll show you biting." And he twists and tangles her into the long night. He is asleep and snoring when later she takes her dustpan and brush and sweeps the spider away.

CRUISE CONTROL

By John Holton

"One hundred … one hundred … one hundred, Greg!"

"I am doing a hundred. You can't read the speedo from that angle. It's an optical illusion."

He eases off the accelerator.

"It's always an optical illusion when you're speeding. You should use the cruise control – we paid for it and you never use it."

"What about the air bags? We paid for them too. Should I choose a solid looking tree to test them out?"

"You just flick a switch, Greg. It's just a very small movement of the index finger. You slow down and flick the switch."

"There is too many bloody switches. You need NASA training to drive this thing. It's like the flight simulator on Apollo 11."

"You haven't even read the owners manual."

He takes both hands off the wheel and holds them in the air.

"Well, line me up and shoot me."

"Greg! Stop it."

"I like a little mystery in my life, okay? A little excitement. Anyway, life's too short to waste reading instruction manuals."

"Oh, and you've got so much else to read haven't you? God, you always make it sound like you're such a bookworm. When did you last read anything other than Inside Football or The Green Guide?"

"Hey, don't knock The Green Guide, Jules. It's the thinking man's TV guide."

"You're such a con artist. Everyone thinks you're this well-read academic – *so* deep and insightful."

"So, academics shouldn't watch TV or like football?"

"Greg, you teach hospitality. It might be called a university but, believe me, there's nothing academic about setting tables."

"So, we're back to the whole *hospitality loser* thing again."

"Those are your words. I don't want to have this stupid argument again. There's nothing wrong with your job.

I'm just saying you're a technophobe – it's always the machines fault."

"Hey, who wanted a new car, anyway?"

"It's like the VCR all over again. How hard is it to tape '*Sex and the City*' on Monday nights? Two buttons, Greg, that's all it takes – easier than a cigarette machine – and what do I get? The English Premier League on SBS."

"There are too many appliances in the world. It exhausts me. Besides, you once said you loved me because I was uncomplicated."

"You can't fight technology, Greg. I don't know why you'd want to when it makes life easier? *Uncomplicated*, did I really say that?" (Pause) "Why are you in such a hurry, anyway? You hate visiting my mum."

"Hey, that's unfair. I've never said that. You're putting words in my mouth."

"You don't have to say it. I only have to mention her name and your eyes roll back in your head."

"When did you last say anything nice about her?"

"She's my mum. It's different when it's your own family. I don't mean any of it – I just want what best for her. At least we still talk."

"It's so unrealistic."

"What is?"

"This whole expectation that everyone in the world should get on with their parents. It's not like we have any choice. It's totally random. Life's too short for..."

"Listen to yourself, Greg: life's too short – life's too short – you never actually *do* anything."

(Pause – road noise)

"And what's this one's name – Abraham? Or was it Ishmaal?"

"His name's Isaac and don't be such a prick about it. She deserves a bit of happiness."

"I knew it was Old Testament. Jewish is he?"

"Mum said he likes to think of himself as a *secular* Jew."

"A secular Jew? Is that like an agnostic Christian? Or a Buddhist with violent tendencies? Gets to enjoy all the Jewish holidays without any of the dogma."

"Don't get on your high horse, Greg. Life may be short but it's not as black and white as you *academics* seem to think."

"Yeah, right."

"Besides, Isaac has his own business, quite successful apparently, so don't go spouting off in front of Mum. She really likes this one. He sounds like he might be right for her."

"Jesus, listen to yourself. Mr Right, eh? Again! Give me strength."

"Left up here – and will you slow down! If you drove a bit slower you'd see the signposts without me having to yell at you."

"And what would be the fun in that, Jules?"

"I love getting out of town. You know, we could have a place out here. A little weekender – something to renovate for when we get older."

"*You?* In the country? You'd go mad – or at least send *me* insane."

"What do you mean?"

"Well, no shops for a start. Twenty four hours out here and you'd be frantically looking for somewhere to swipe your plastic cards."

"That is so typical – just because you've got a hang up about credit. You and your dad's tight-arsed protestant work ethic. Don't try and lump your guilt on me."

"Think about it Jules, honestly, you'd be bored witless. No cafes, no gym on Thursdays, bad TV reception."

"You know, I'm starting to think that you really don't know anything about me. You think I'm so one-dimensional."

"Why are we arguing about this? This is never, ever going to happen. It's pointless. This whole drive is like a dial-a-*f**king*-argument."

(Pause)

"I could learn a craft. I could spin wool or –"

"- write bush verse?"

"You can be a sarcastic prick sometimes. Can't you ever just let go and speculate on hypotheticals for the fun of it. For fun? Remember fun, Greg? It was all the rage last century before we got married."

"Life's too short for –"

"Shut up, Greg. Just – shut – up."

(Pause)

"You'd drive your mother to insanity, you know that. Not that you'd need to take her very far."

"Mum's changed a lot since Dad died, even if certain people refuse to see it. We could spend more time together.

Get to know Isaac better."

"Aren't you rushing this Isaac thing a little? I mean, how longs' it been – six weeks?"

"It's four weeks longer than Clive. That has to be a positive. Can you overtake this guy with the trailer, the exhaust fumes are giving me a headache."

"I can't pass here, it's double lines."

"Why do you do this to me, Greg? For the last hour you've been Michael sodding Schumaker, now all of a sudden you won't overtake a car?"

"Settle, *Hon*. I'll do it when it's safe."

"Don't Hon me – I hate it. This is where the winding road starts. If you don't do it now we'll be stuck behind him for the next ten kilometres. If I get a migraine the days over, you know that."

"I'll pull over then."

"No! Don't pull over. Mum said lunch is at 12.30. We can't afford to stop – the black forest cake'll be festering in the boot."

"Look, what if I just hang back a little and see if – what are you doing with the phone?"

"I'm going to call him."

"Who?"

"This McNally guy – the gardener."

"You can't *phone* him."

"Of course I can. Why would he have his number plastered all over his trailer if he didn't want people to phone him?"

"It's not like you're ringing to have your lawns mowed. Christ Jules, you're seriously losing the plot. It's not that big a deal."

"I'll just ask him nicely if he wouldn't mind pulling over to let us pass. Why would he have a problem with that?"

"You don't know who he is? There's probably some seriously scary tools in that trailer. He could be the psychotic Irish gardener from hell."

"It's ringing."

" – or a serial hedge burner who comes around at three in the morning to – "

"Hello, is this McNally's Gardening? Sorry to bother you Mr McNally, this is Julie Sutcliffe. We're travelling behind you in the burgundy coloured … what make of car is it, Greg?"

"A Honda Accord. *Who* didn't read the manual?"

"We're travelling behind you in the burgundy Honda Accord and we're a little pushed for time, I was wondering if you wouldn't mind … oh, that'd be great, we'd really appreciate it. Thanks so much, Mr McNally – Happy gardening!"

"I don't believe it."

"See? You just need to have a little faith in people. There's a lot of good in the world if you just make an effort."

"Now he's waving to us – bloody hell."

"Can we stop talking now, Greg? Just enjoy the drive?" She pushes a CD into the player.

"For the rest of the drive I'm listening to Enya."

"Is it dead? It looks dead."

"I can't tell. It doesn't seem to be moving. Its eyes are open."

"That doesn't mean anything. Lots of dead things have their eyes open … shit, look at the car!"

"Can we still drive it?"

"I think it just stalled, but look at the damage. That whole front panel's going to need replacing. The headlight's f**ked. It could cost thousands. F**king Enya."

"What? What are you talking about?"

"Bad things always happen when you listen to Enya."

"Greg! It moved."

"What?"

"The kangaroo. It moved, I swear."

"It's probably just nerves twitching. I'm sure it's dead – the way its eyes are staring like that."

"Look, there it is again. Did you see it?"

"It's the pouch. Jules, there's something moving in the pouch. Jesus, it's got a joey."He rubs both hands through his hair.

"What should we do? Do we try and rescue it?"

"I don't know! You're the one who watches Animal Hospital. Can they live without a mother? Christ, Jules, I've killed its mother."

"Hey, there was nothing you could do. She was just there in front of the car – I didn't see her either. But we can't leave this little guy here on the side of the road."

"Get the rug off the back seat – and the tea towels you wrapped around the cake." "What are you going to do?"

"I don't know – prepare a picnic?"

"What do you mean?"

"It was a joke, Jules. I'm a little out of my depth here, okay. I'm used to serving them up as bush tucker in the Uni bistro."

"I can't believe I'm doing this. It's so warm inside – like she's got a hot water bottle in there."

"Just be careful it doesn't scratch you. It's a wild animal after all – and those tea towels are only thin."

"I don't think it's capable. It's trembling more than I am. The poor little thing's scared shitless."

"Have you got it?"

"I think I've got my hands around the front paws. I'll just hold him for a moment. Jules, it's tiny – like a stuffed toy."

Silence. They make eye contact – smile nervously at each other.

"What should I do?"

"Hold the rug up close. Ready? Here we go – it's okay, little fella, don't kick."

"He's so small. Look how tiny he is."

"Have you got hold of it? Careful."

"Oh Greg, he's so cute."

"Wrap it up tightly, so it can't kick itself free."

"Listen to you. You sound like you do this every day."

"Give me a break, Jules."

"No, I meant it as a compliment. My very own Steve Irwin. I like it."

"I think I must be in shock. My heart's going like the clappers."

"Look at him Greg, he's snuggling in – like a little baby."

"Don't go all clucky on me. It is pretty cute, I'll give you that."

"What do we do now?"

"I don't know. There must be someone out here who handles this sort of thing."

There is silence, punctuated by a magpies' warble, then a distant hum.

"Is that a car? There's a car coming."

"Ha … it's your friend, McNally. Will I flag him over or just hit the redial button?"

"Is he from around here?"

"I'm not sure. He just said there was a place about twenty k's up the road where we could leave the little bloke for Wildlife Rescue to collect." Said he had their number in his ute and would phone ahead."

"God, he must think we're a couple of neurotics from the big smoke."

"I think we did okay for a couple of neurotics, don't you?"

"Yeah, I guess we did. Look at his wet little nose. God, he's so cute. I wish we could just turn around and take him back home with us."

"I think the body corporate probably has rules about native wildlife in the building. I can just see you taking him for a hop around Albert Park."

Laughter.

"Maybe we could get a cat?"

"Or a gerbil."

"A what?"

"I saw it on TV. One of those shows about unusual pets. It's kind of a pocket-sized kangaroo – well, sort of."

"A gerbil?"

(Long, thoughtful pause)

"What you said earlier – about a place in the country – it's not *that* far-fetched – not really."

"Look at his eye lashes, Greg. They're so long, so perfect."

"Just something small, I mean. A little miner's cottage or something."

"Do you think it's a he or a she? I wonder how you tell with kangaroos?"

"I don't know. I suppose it's like a dog."

"Or a gerbil. You know, there're people who spend their whole lives doing this."

"What?"

"Looking after orphaned animals. Hand rearing kangaroos and wombats and things. Imagine."

"Yeah, imagine what their houses smell like."

"Seriously, Greg. I can see how you'd get attached – hey, McNally's turning up ahead. This place we're going must be pretty close to Mum's."

"We won't be so late after all. What shape was the black forest cake in when you checked?"

"It wasn't exactly a shape. You could probably lick some off the spare tyre but-"She stops mid-sentence – nuzzles her face into the joey's fur.

"Are you crying, Jules? Hey, hey, don't cry. It's all right – it's just a cake. Just flour and eggs."

"It's not the cake." Sobs. "I don't care about the stupid cake – or the car."

"What, then? What is it?"

"I keep thinking about that poor kangaroo … but I'm sort of happy at the same time. I can't explain … it's stupid." He leans across – rubs her thigh with his free hand.

"Well don't get too happy or you'll drown the little bugger." She sniffs back tears. He wipes her nose with his sleeve. She smiles.

"A miner's cottage? It has a nice ring to it – like Snow White." The car slows – both deep in thought.

"Jesus, look who's pulling into your mum's driveway."

"You're kidding. *Isaac* McNally? No way."

"I feel like I should be more surprised."

"Irish father … Jewish mother? Is that how it works?"

"*A secular, Irish Catholic, gardening Jew?*" He laughs. "I like it – I like it a lot. If he's a football fan, he'll be perfect. Hell, I might marry him myself."

She wipes the last tears away on the palm of her hand.

"What?" Why are smiling at me like that? Greg, stop it, you're making me nervous."

"It's just you, cuddling that damn joey … look at you both – it's like you've found each other."

SHELL PAST AJAR

By Stella Prideaux

Cars drive on either side of the broken white line, like the foot of a sewing machine stitching together both lanes. Broken (separated) white stitches upon pavement. On the underside of the road the stitches would fall in the gaps up above.
The visible side of the road:
Stitch gap stitch gap stitch gap...
The invisible underneath of the road:
gap stitch gap stitch gap stitch...
The thread snaking.
The road is balanced and together.

STITCH

I am still in my wetsuit, dripping and I wonder how vinegar is more corrosive than the salt water these abalones lived in. We go snorkelling and he catches them to eat. He beats them to death with a mallet because it apparently makes them more tender. He says that's how you're supposed to prepare them, but I steer clear. I just like their shells. He says if I polish the coarse back of them with vinegar it will scratch away to reveal the mother-of-pearl underneath, so that the whole shell is mother-of-pearl. I lie on the sand and stick abalones onto my wetsuited stomach. They suction on to it, as though it's the rock they've just been rudely pried from with a diver's knife.

STITCH

He is stitching together the road as we drive past a sign depicting black circle with a black line through it. It means no speed limit. The black markings represent no, the white background must represent speed.

We are playing a game where you have to predict what kind of wave the people in oncoming traffic will give – called "waver, lazy-waver, or wanker". There hasn't been any oncoming traffic for a couple of hours.

A V-shaped flock of birds enters my vision from the right in slow motion. It looks like he can see them so I don't react. There is a sudden thump on the windscreen in front of me, followed by silence. I begin to laugh. He says that vegetarians aren't supposed to laugh at road kill and puts on the wipers. The bird rubs up and down the windscreen like a washcloth, with something resembling an intestine trailing behind, the entire car screams and I feel like we're in one of those mock-horror (right genre for *Scary Movie*) movies. Shock humour.

He cleans it off at the next service station, at a corporate yellow shell and the man I pay for petrol tells me I'm lucky we didn't hit a hawk," 'cause they can break your whole windscreen. As big as large dogs, they are."

STITCH

You wake me up by having one of your sneezing fits in the front seat and I keep reading the Jeff Noon story, The Cabinet of Night Unlocked. He's stitching the road together and you're reading my Ode to Dinner.

Dinner:
Shell pasta in a jar
Shell future in a jar
Shell past in a jar

Shell past ajar
Hungry hands into
glass
shells that break between
teeth like hard plastic
waiting and watching water boil
above flaming metho
the bottle is half empty
not half full
no use crying over spilt spirits
methylated spirits
methylated replacements:
alcohol, deodorant, petrol
"Petrol?" I joke
"Petrol!" she exclaims
and I am holding my *pink joke*
my *pink liqueur*
"Did you know *petrol* was *pink*?"
"Always thought it was brown"
Petrol holds a pink secret in cities
pink lemonade
like in old movies
it is my job to
Pour pink posh lemonade and
her job to cook
black smoke curls up in the dusk
the *sharp* taste of
petrol
am I really tasting it?
it tasted sharp
at first
the sauce for the pasta tastes
strong

"Are you spinning?"
"It's more like figure-eighting"
"Or swinging"
"Yeah, swinging"
"I want to be cremated, doused
in *pink* lemonade and clear spirits.
And my epitaph will read:
"My compliments to the chef""
"Shut the f**k up"
f**k-up
but
we're laughing
at a stupid
Pink, mock-posh *punch*-line joke
laughing at a grave that
says:
"What doesn't kill me will only make me stronger"
laughing
because
things are so much funnier when
they're not funny
laughing together
on a garden swing
swinging together
in a timeless ad for
pink lemonade
cropped by a white fuzzy circle
enclosing large white American teeth
swinging
holding chilled cans
with a corporate yellow shell
logo upon them
with the colouring of the *golden arches*

crushed shells
sand
glass
a wooden spoon
like a paint brush
painted the outside of our pot black with thick velvety
charcoal
the inside still silver like
mother-of-pearl
inside
abalone shells
we eat pearls for dinner
glass
sand
crushed shells
shell past ajar

STITCH

This *Ode to Dinner* is not polished. I have abalone shells, a bottle of vinegar and your tooth brush, I am trying to polish shells so that the entire back is mother-of-pearl without polishing too far in certain areas and creating holes.

STITCH

I am stitching together the road while he tests us on our Australian slang from his guidebook.
"Woop Woop?"
"Out in the middle of nowhere."
Distances are different out here. The land is so flat that we can see several different storms at once.

Melbourne's summer storms would come to *us* – a number of brooding hot days culminating in water. At the coastline, the sea would turn a light fluorescent green, the sky a dark purple, lower than usual, building pressure – till you felt like pricking the inflated clouds with a pin.

"Bitumen?"

"Umm, like, black roads."

"Gravel tar roads."

"Yep, Cark it?"

"To die."

Here storms are something you drive into and out of. They are cylindrical sections of streaked and dark sky. One cylinder slightly to the left of the road out the front windscreen and one directly to the right.

STITCH

I am polishing abalone shells with vinegar. It corrodes the coarse back of the shell to reveal the mother-of-pearl beneath.

STITCH

I am stitching together the road and humming to the Janis Joplin version of *Summertime*.

"Wanker," she says

"Yeah, wanker," I agree.

I pull over amongst a surprising scarcity of tourists. As you do with all landmarks, we invent our own myths for Uluru.

"It looks like a giant termite mound dating from the beginning of time, housing the king and queen termite, who are quietly biding their time until the human race has created a world-wide desert," she says.

"I think after the aliens had created the precision of the pyramids they wanted to delve into more abstract style of art," he says.

Hers paid attention to what it looks like and his sounded intellectual.

I am trying to think of a myth as we escape the closed air of the car and walk across sand to Uluru's base.

I'm finding it hard to talk because I'm thinking too much about the category each spoken sentence is cast in. Visual or intellectual or...

STITCH

On average it only rains here twice a year. Storm clouds tremble over the top of the rock, both days and we're spared the moral dilemma of whether to climb it or not. Apparently, when it's closed like this, keen Japanese tourists who've flown in for one day especially to climb the Rock ("I came, I saw, I conquered") scale it anywhere they can, risking life or limb and the 1000 dollar fine (that we've characteristically noticed).

STITCH

According to the guidebook the local Aboriginals call the people climbing the rock the "minga mob", minga meaning ant. Ants invading a termite mound. Ants creeping across a discarded piece of abstract art. I imagine the climbing people wearing the rock down like the kissed feet of St Peter in Rome, or perhaps just wearing a linear pathway into it. I'm finding it hard to talk.

The weather feels nice after the heat of the North.

STITCH

Ants taste spicy. I didn't realise it was an ant till I extracted the spicy point from a mouthful of food.

STITCH

I am polishing the coarse back of abalone shells with vinegar to make the entire shell mother-of-pearl, but I keep polishing too far in areas and creating holes. The shell is all fragile, brittle and splotchy.

STITCH

Apparently in REM sleep your body has no temperature control. As a survival mechanism, when you're in extreme heat or cold, you do not enter REM sleep. It is outside such sleep, on the more surface levels of sleep, that you dream.

STITCH

"Are your feet touching the coral?"
I like to have bare feet so I can touch the landscape I walk through
He is talking in his sleep, or floating in his sleep
Floating above coral and trying to protect his feet

STITCH

She is stitching together a blank road running through blank territory, while I stare at an incomprehensible map.

"Have you ever really thought about how, on maps, ocean names just float out in the middle of no where?" He is staring thoughtfully out the window. "There's the turn you idiot," she says.

She brakes and my thoughts run in time to the indicator. "Which noise do you find most irritating when trying to sleep?" I ask, "an even, methodical sound like a wrist watch ticking, or a sound that you wait for and hope won't come again, like a dripping tap?"

He has pulled out his camera.

"What *are* you doing?"

"What? They won't believe me back home about these huge trucks, road trains rather. I suppose you need things like that over here, what with everything being so far apart. I mean, petrol has to be heaps cheaper out here, otherwise no one would get anywhere."

A voice over the radio, "In recent news, the current generation of truck drivers are all ageing to the point that there will soon be a national shortage of workers in the area…"

"That's true, you never do see young truck drivers, ey?"

STITCH

When I was little, too hot to fall asleep and too lazy to get up – I would flip my pillow over and over so I could stick my arm underneath where it hadn't been warmed by my body, until I fell asleep.

STITCH

I am trying to polish shells so that the entire back is mother-of-pearl. Most of my shells are broken and she's already whinging about the mess.

STITCH

The road is unravelling.

We judge whether we're safe to drive, by whether we are reconstructing a TAC ad. The familiarity gives us caution. I wind down the window, like they do in the ads to stay awake. In the TAC advertisements the drivers are never dodging kangaroos that jump suddenly from the darkness into the light of high beams.

He wants to catch a crocodile whilst he's in Australia, like Steve Irwin.

"I've been told small dogs provide good bait."

"We should skin it and make a surfboard-cover for her birthday."

"Yeah, perfect shape, the surfboard can like…feed into its mouth."

"Totally! We could open a whole crocodile surfing…label"

"Yeh!…called 'A Croc Stole my Surfboard'."

"Perfect!"

A large dark cylinder must have moved sideways, as we are driving through rain, the wipers waving rhythmically like a turning pillow.

"What the f**k?"

"Either I'm hallucinating or there are two camels on the road."

STITCH

He is walking along the beach collecting those coloured smooth fragments of glass – almost frosted, sanded down shards – of beer bottles, wine bottles, discarded at different levels of intoxication. They make a soft grainy clink together as he places them in his palm.

STITCH

When I'm drunk I always throw car keys in the air, (rhythmically not randomly) to hear them make the noise of wind-chimes. Rhythmically and evenly they make the noise of wind-chimes. High-pitched chiming in the air and a lower-pitched staccato as they hit my hand. The air, my hand, the air, my hand, occasionally hitting the ground and splintering my rhythm.

STITCH

You are sitting on the bonnet correcting spelling and grammar and giving me suggestions. You use one of my abalone shells as an ashtray. I pick it up and rub the uneven ridges underneath with my fingertip. The ash sits neatly centred in the mother-of-pearl, with neat beads of holes bordering one side where the abalone's small tentacles would emerge. You concentrate more easily when you smoke.

UNSTITCH

I can't hear it, but I know that an indicator is ticking rhythmically beneath the chaos somewhere, creating comfort. The car hit a tree. Not slowly and with a crumple like a new car would have, but colliding with it in one short violent staccato and rebounding about an inch in time with all our heads. I am sitting in the backseat with a whole lot of crushed abalone shells still holding your toothbrush. The shells were crushed before we hit the tree.

She is laughing at the fact that her last words could have been "take your foot off the brake!" I don't really know what mine would have been. I wasn't really speaking English. I can't really speak now either, because I'm laughing so hard.

He keeps saying what the f**k over and over.

STITCH

I was dressing black markings in colour. I was dressing black markings in colour. The black markings represent *No*, the white background must represent *Speed*.

Try turning the *No* into the background and the Speed into the foreground.

The weaving white pathways look like snail trails.

STITCH

I reach down and pull a white stitch in the pavement and the road we've sewn together so far bunches up like a drawstring so that we're at the beginning and the end at the same time.

*stitch*glasss*stitch*sand*stitch*crushedshells...

*st*glsch*sat*crshll

Shell past ajar

ROAD TRIP

By Andrew Hutchinson

When it happened, Jen's face just looked at me, I remember, like it was all my fault. And it was. And when I pushed my eyes shut till they burned and tried to shake it away, her staring at me just stayed. Still shot. Up ahead the road was straight and empty, the only noise my feet tapping along the concrete. There was no one here. It was raining but only like a layer, a veil across the real world. My chest ached when I rubbed it, but I didn't want to look. And I stumbled across my own feet and on.

Rewind

It was weeks, maybe a month, when Jen had said she wouldn't see me any more. Not couldn't, but wouldn't. It flashed my mind across all the time we'd been us. She said it started the time she thought she was pregnant, that's what got her to thinking. That was the night I walked along the streetlights of the city and cried into broken bottles and concrete gutters.

I climbed stairs to the top of the commission flats and watched the world flicker by through the darkness.

My friend Sam had dragged me out again, through bright daylight and sun. Sam has told me to move on and taken me on drunken nights where the lights and buildings became a blur. We'd gone on road trips to nowhere and slept, all folded up, in car seats beside the freeway. We'd staggered along sandy beaches in moonlight yelling to people we used to know, as if they'd hear it bouncing off the ripples of the ocean. He had put his arm around me and said that "there's more out there for you", his hand waving across the painted picture horizon.

He told me once, as we threw stones across night covered river, about a car accident. Sam said it was so loud, louder than he imagined it would be and how he couldn't remember clearly what happened. Like still shots from a film in his head. He said he felt warm blood on his forehead like sweat, but not like sweat. In his hair too. He scanned his fingertips across his skin for damage. Some of his teeth had broken and, pushing them together, he felt the gaps and jagged piece against his gums. Through the shattered glass and chipped paint across the framework, the road ahead was quiet, dead. Peaceful. Sam said, this is worse than being without someone. This, being alive, is something to appreciate. Sam threw a stone into the night, watched it disappear into the water.

Fast Forward

When Jen called again it felt as though my heart grew in my chest, like a balloon filled and released. She called and said she didn't know what to say. We pretended nothing had happened and tried to talk normally. We talked about nothing. And it was perfect. She said she wanted to see me and we met in the city that week.

"Have you slept with anyone?" she asked. I asked back, but not because I wanted to know. I needed to know. She said things like her dog misses me and she touched my hand. She said things and I didn't know whether to laugh. Or cry. The crowds of the city kept it away though. All of it.

She sat in my car and looked around. She changed the CD and asked about us. Said she missed me too. My fingers gripped the steering wheel. I told her I would do anything for her. She said we couldn't be together. No matter what I said after, she would not change. A sad song on the radio.

My body weighed me down and I looked at her staring out the open window of the passenger seat, running her fingers across the wind, the world flashing by her. A car horn screaming nearby. Closer. Louder.

What I remember is seeing the world flash by Jen's window, the headlights of a truck through mine. What I remember is the roof folding in like a V shape and the world losing sense and direction. The glass in the air was shattered into tiny granules of safe, squared-off, diamonds. The music stopped, water splashed across my face and the seatbelt choked me back. The steering wheel tearing at my chest. What I remember is Jen's hair flying and smashing in the air, her arms collapsing with the car. What I remember is screaming her name.

The road is by my face, liquid running across the concrete and paint, glass, splashed all over. I force my way out and grab at my head, feel for blood. At the other side of the broken metal is Jen, upside down and bent up. She has her eyes open, but not really. She looks at me. She stares at me. I touch her cheek. She stares at me.

Play

A car drifts along the road; I see it from a distance. A young couple stops in front of me, in the misty rain, open the door for me to get in. I sit in the backseat and grab a blanket, wrap it around me. They smile and ask where I'm going. I make up somewhere. My chest aches, like my ribs are smashed. Maybe they are. Sweat rolls across my forehead, but it's not sweat. We come round the bend where cars have stopped by a smashed truck and a broken metal frame of a car. Jen is still inside. The driver of the young couple's car looks at me in the mirror, notices the blood above my eye. In my mind, I beg for him to look away.

"You weren't in this accident here were you?" When I close my eyes, close them till they burn, I see Jen's face, staring. Just staring at me. And it's my fault. I pull the blanket to cover my neck and feel tears across my face, try to breathe normally. My chest burns.

"No," I cry to him, his eyes staring in the rear-view mirror, the women rubbernecking to look at me, at the accident.

"No," I cry louder. My lips stick together. Blood on my forehead. "No, no no." Cover my eyes.

ROAD TO MUMBANNAR

By Marica Salpietro

9:00 PM

Should have known I'd get the Mumbannar route again. "You're our best driver, Molly. I knew you wouldn't say no," Wally said, slapping me on the back and throwing me the keys to the truck. Before I had a chance to tell him that this would be the ninth week in a row that I would be doing the same route, he was half way up the driveway. I cursed him under my breath and climbed up into the truck. Mental note to self: Tell Wally I refuse to do Mumbannar route again. Second mental note to self: Read Dr Phil before telling Wally I refuse to do Mumbannar route again.

9:03 PM

Pre-departure checklist: Fuel? Check. Dinner? Check. Daryl. Daryl? DARYL!

9:15 PM

Found Daryl at the back of the depot with nose stuck in garbage bin. Had to yank him away by the collar with a piece of former cow still dangling from mouth. Not a pretty sight.

9:30 PM

We are on our way, Daryl. Only nine hours to go! Ah, yes, nine hours will go as fast as lightning. Just you and me buddy.

All alone. Nothing but pitch-black ahead. A bit of deep-and-meaningful time. Time to ourselves.

What shall we discuss tonight? World politics or the ozone issue? Oh, yes, you're right. Discussed them last week, didn't we? So, Dazza, what do you think about the legalisation of euthanasia?

9:40 PM

Realise that I have been debating the pros and cons about euthanasia with someone who can't help scratching himself and then licks himself clean. Right, talkback radio it is.

9:41 PM

No talkback radio on tonight. Humph!

9:42 PM

Refuse to listen to rap.

9:43 PM

Refuse to listen to Kylie, Britney, J. Lo.

9:45 PM

What station is this? Turkish News FM? Would be okay if spoke Turkish. 9:50 PM Right. No more radio. I will sit here and spend the time producing quality thoughts.

10:00 PM

Production of quality thoughts will start soon.

10:01 PM

What do I talk to myself about? I already know everything about myself. Kinda have to in this sort of job. You have to be your own best friend. Never rely on anyone except yourself, that way you'll never get let down. Learnt that the hard way, though. Tony always said he was going down to the pub with the boys, but what he really meant was he was seeing Tanya Robbins for a bit of fun on the side. Bastard. All men are the same. Should have listened to Mum.

10:05 PM

Although, if I had listened to Mum, I'd be wearing a frilly apron, blow-drying hair and taking out rollers at the salon. Mum always said hairdressing was a "respectable trade for a young lady". She encouraged me by buying me chest-enhanced Barbies with long hair. She wanted me to plait and blow-dry their hair. The year I gave Barbie an Afro, Mum's dream of me joining the salon suddenly vanished.

10:30 PM

Ah, smell that fresh air! Nothing like the country air to get you going. Will be heading onto the Mumbannar Highway soon. That'll be good. All the other routes take the highway for a good 20km before they turn. Ah, I think I can see Mick's old metallic beast now. I think I'll honk my horn when I get close enough.

10:35 PM

Mick just honked back. What a guy. Perhaps I'll just ask him how his night's going on the radio.

10:40 PM
"Hey Molly, rear looking great as always. He he. Over."

10:42 PM

"You doing Mumbannar again? Jesus, Molly, you really need to get a life, honey. Over."

10:45 PM

Turned radio off. What did he mean I need to get a life? I have a life, thank you very much. We have a great life, don't we Daryl? Daryl?

10:46 PM

Daryl is busy wagging his tail, watching the procession of trucks turning off into the night. Humph!

11:00 PM

Well of course I have a life. I love my life. What's there not to love? A great job – well, OK, a good job.

At least I have all the time in the world to do what I want. I can just keep on going, doing what I want, when I want. That's freedom. Why, if I feel like a hot jam doughnut I could pull over right now and have one. How many other jobs will let you do that?

11:10 PM

Don't have any jam doughnuts. Will open the Tim Tams instead.

11:20 PM

No more Tim Tams. Humph! How did that happen?

11:45 PM

Spent last 25 minutes thinking about Mick's comment. Sure, truckin' isn't an average female profession. Just because it is a male-dominant profession doesn't mean I am any less a person. I earned this job. I studied for it. I spent five years at uni studying mechanics and engineering. How many other women can point out the hydraulic cylinders? Or test the level of oil with precision? Or change a tyre without flashing her leg to oncoming traffic?

MIDNIGHT

I always stood out. As a kid, I copped a lot from the other girls. While they were dressed in cotton cardigans and woollen skirts, I wore blue overalls and flannel shirts. The other girls rubbed lotion on their hands, while I was rubbing oil and grease. On my ninth birthday, Mum said to me I should have been a boy. She bought me "Barbie's First Campervan". To which I asked her if I could exchange the campervan for a Land Rover. From that year on I got Tonka trucks.

12:07 AM

The best birthday was the big 18. Nine o'clock sharp I was at VicRoads ready to take to the road like a seagull eyeing hot chips. Needless to say, I passed with flying colours. Honest. Okay, okay, there were a few small hiccups. I crossed three lanes without doing a head check and instead of turning on the indicator I switched on the windscreen wipers. Oh yeah and as I leaned down to pull the seat forward I beeped the horn with my right breast. A little something for the driving instructor to share at the Christmas party, no doubt.

12:15 AM

Ever since I got my licence, I haven't stopped driving. I love that feeling of being in control of an oversized vehicle. You're God when you drive, you can go anywhere. You sit up high above anyone else on the road and see things from a different perspective. You forget about all your troubles and concentrate on the road ahead. The sky lit up with millions of stars, the stillness of remote dirt roads, the soft night breeze blowing in your eyes. It's so peaceful and relaxing...

12:16 AM

Oops! First road kill for the night. A wombat on a suicide mission.

12:40 AM

Not a good night for wombats. Another one jumped out in front of me wanting to end its life. Honked my horn in bid to scare it, but to no avail. It must have been a suicide pact.

1:30 AM

Mmm, time for din dins. Where did I put lunch box? Ah, there it is. Daryl! Down boy! Stop licking my face. I'm trying to drive! Daryl, down. GET OFF ME!

1:35 AM

Daryl has sulked off on the back seat. He'll get over it. I told him he could sit back up the front when he is ready to behave. No use pouting, you have to learn, old boy.

2:00 AM

Poor guy is feeling horrible. Look at the way his mouth drops with sadness. He has his paws on top of his droopy ears, as if trying to hide from the world. Ah, geez, why do I feel so horrible?

2:20 AM

I'll be the bigger person here and throw him a biscuit.

2:30 AM

I'm sorry, buddy. Come on, up the front. That's a good boy. Yes, you're a very good boy… no, that doesn't mean you can lick – [coughing out fur ball].

3:05 AM

Ah, nearly there, Daryl old boy. Nearly made it. This is the best time of night you know, nobody around. Feels like we're the only two people left on earth. All right, the only person and dog left.

3:10 AM

I remember my first trip into Mumbannar a couple of years back. Daryl was only a pup, yapping and jumping. This was just after I found out Tony was getting his gear off every Saturday night with his "mates at the pub". I went and saw Wally, who gave me the job on the spot and I did my first route that night. It was the Mumbannar Route. What a liberating drive! The sound of the engine choking up the dirt road and around the sharp bends which Wally warned me about. I just drove and drove, with the knowledge that my cheating fiancé was further and further away. Surprisingly, hit a lot of road kill that night. I finally arrived at Mumbannar in the early hours of the morning. There was an old tin shed by the side of the road with a faded sign that detailed the population of the town. The town was so insignificant in size, the local joke was that there were more people in the local cemetery than living. So why is it that I keep coming back?

4:00 AM

Mumbannar is such a tiny town that Australia Post wiped it off the postal map. It shares its postcode with the town Heywood, 50km away. The population of 200 wasn't too impressed with that decision. It's still causing confusion and mail is always going astray. I can still see good old Marjorie Davies marching up to the local post office, waving an envelope and saying, "You mongrels have taken our postcode from underneath us!"

4:30 AM

Marjorie Davies will be stirring in her sleep right about now, her alarm buzzing beside her. "Molly'll be here soon," she'll be thinking. "Thank goodness for our Molly." She'll hoist herself out of bed and she'll be clambering in the kitchen ready to bake her famous ginger and walnut cookies. Mmmm, can you smell them, Daryl?

4:31 AM

Daryl? What is it Buddy? What's the matter? Stop jumping round now, just calm down. What is it?

4:34 AM

Truck comes to a complete stop. Open the door and Daryl frantically scrambles on top of me to get out. Call of nature.

4:40 AM

That's better, eh Daryl? Off we go, old buddy.

5:00 AM

One hour left! Nearly there Daryl, can you smell those ginger and walnut treats waiting for us? "You drove all that way, aren't you a dear," Marjorie will say. "Now don't be shy, look they're still warm. Help yourself, Molly. You too Daryl, oh … oh, not all of them, you're a hungry fella aren't you, Daryl?" Daryl doesn't need any encouragement, do you, buddy? Marjorie will be waiting outside the post office to see us turning up the main street. She always has. She'll still have the curlers in her hair from the night before, her face freshly painted with make-up.

5:10 AM

I met Marjorie on my very first night on the job. Marjorie was waiting at the post office dressed in nothing more than a long white nightgown and a blanket around her shoulders. "My, you don't look much like the last truckie," were her first words. "You're a woman." It was tradition for someone in the town to welcome the truckies, to show their appreciation and gratitude for the long drive. We were their link to the outside world, delivering newspapers, medical supplies, fresh vegetables, firewood, canned goods and the mail. Everyone always came up to greet me and gathered around, eager to see what parcels I had for them. I was like the popular girl at high school, or the favourite child. Everybody wanted a piece of me. What a feeling that gave me inside! Nothing else compares to the feeling of being wanted and needed. It was always worth the long drive.

5:43 AM

Everyone will have treats for you today, Daryl. You'll be spoilt today, won't you, buddy? Whoa! Down boy, calm down now. We're nearly there. Daryl, stop it! Just sit still. Calm down. I'm trying to drive. Sit! Sit! Stay! What are you doing? Daryl! Daryl! Stop that! Get Off! I said enough! Daryl! DARYL! GET OFF ME! WHOA... OH GOD, NO! DARYLLLLLLLLLLLLLLLLLL!

9:00 AM

"Molly, this is Wally. Over ... why haven't you signed in? Where the hell are you? Do you copy? Over... Molly, what the hell is going on? What's happened? Marjorie Davies called to say you never made it... Molly? Do you copy? Are you still on the Road to Mumbannar?"

THE ROAD TO FISHERMAN'S PEAK

By Jack Johnson

It was one of those nights. I couldn't sleep, no matter what I tried I couldn't shut my mind off. I felt cold, tired and a little bit edgy, which is no surprise. Not being able to doze off is like drinking too much coffee, especially if it's night after night. The cold breeze was rattling the blinds, the curtains were taking the shape of the invisible force that goes wherever it wants, whenever it wants, as its own will. Its own will … do you think it has a will? I thought to myself, I mean did it really want to come into my window?… my window … just to see what I'm doing … did I say that? Well, it has a life of its own, I thought, you can't see it … yet you can see where it's going and what it's doing. Here I go again, anything that comes into my head to stop me from sleeping. It's just the bloody wind, but is it? I heard a voice inside me say…

I slowly pulled back the covers, sat up and rubbed my eyes. So cold that I could feel my body go rigid from lack of warmth, my breathing was shallow and rapid, my arms clutching my body, attempting to somehow keep the cold at bay. I sat up and reached for the jumper at the end of the bed. Pulled it over my head and stepped out. Tripping on the books I had piled on the floor. Ow! My big toe was throbbing from the pain of The Complete Works of Shakespeare. I got to the window and closed it tight, ha! I felt triumphant, I had locked It out … but it didn't seem to care. I heard it again, it appeared to be laughing at me and I realised, I was the one who was locked in. The wind was having the time of its life, even making fun of me, showing me it wasn't confined. Maybe it wanted me to come out, maybe that's what the wind was trying to tell me...come out and play, you can be as free as me. You just have to believe...

Hmm... I thought, I mean it's just going to be another sleepless night. Maybe I could go for a drive. I mean it's not like I have to be anywhere tomorrow morning. I've been moping around for the last week thinking about her. Tonight is the anniversary of the so-called disappearance. I winced at the pain it caused me to think about MJ. The guilt and despair not knowing what became of her, if only... No I'm not going to go there, I fought off the familiar thought pattern. I hurriedly put my jeans on, got my wallet, jacket and car keys, locked up the house got through my gate and hopped into my car.

The keys were in, without thinking I was already driving off accepting the challenge of the wind. It had spoken to me and I was responding. I flew down the highway racing away from the comfort of my prison that I called home. Here I was the master, I could be like the wind. Go where I want, do what I want. I wound down the window so I could hear it, smell it. It was almost sexual. Arousing an energy within me that had long disappeared, the driving force that excites you and challenges your fears. I can't remember when I felt so alive.

Somehow I had been given a chance to be different, to go down an unknown path, not that I knew where I was going, or where I'd end up. All I knew was that I had entered into the land of the living again! I had spent so many nights trapped in that room. The wind had taunted me before, yet I didn't know that it was trying to communicate to me. Back then I was so caught up in my world, unable to see what I could really become; can I be just like the invisible force? To drive into the night, along the wind-whipped road, not caring what my destination is. The only objective is to be free.

I was following the path the wind was taking. It hadn't finished with me yet, leading me somewhere I know not where, not that I cared, I was happy to have a purpose. A reason to escape my confines, to be on the road chasing the wind. It was easy enough to keep up, almost as if some plan was hatching.

I had been travelling for at least 45 minutes and had reached the edge of the city. The houses were getting further and further apart. A few lights would twinkle here and there. The night sky looked black compared to the blue hues from the city that I had just left. Looking up into the night, I could see the stars were brighter out here and still the wind kept up its song for me. I could swear it was talking or singing to me in its own kind of way. In my head I could hear it, or maybe I was imagining it, saying: come, come to me...

I just passed the turn off for Fisherman's Peak. The old sign was still standing, the paint cracked and chipped, grass growing up around the base with clumps of weeds, hiding the trail that used to be as well-worn as my favourite 501's. I slowed down to a stop. I could see something glistening just to the left of the sign. As if it was hiding. I could smell the jasmine wafting over from the bushes behind it, mixed with the pungent smell of the river. The watering hole for not only the local wildlife, but also a nice little fishing spot and not a bad one I might add. I can remember catching a few barramundi from that place many a time with Mary Jane, but that was then.

A tear came to my eye as I sat in my ute at the side of the road thinking about the times when this place had happier days. If only I knew what happened that night, maybe this old riverbank would still be humming with activity today. There was always a bunch of kids swimming up at the north end, jumping off the cliff. Screaming at the top of their lungs, "Move it or lose it! Here I come!" And then there was that sweet night when I had stumbled up here with MJ, a little drunk after our first real date.

We had worked with each other all through the first term of school together. She was the science teacher and I was the librarian at the local high school. God it was so hard to keep it down every time she came near me I got a woody. Thank Christ I had a bench to hide behind. She told me later that she could tell that something was up, said if I never asked her out, she was going to jump me in the car park. I can still see her face now, glistening in the moonlight. When suddenly...

I heard a snap in the bushes. Huh, what was that? Probably just some bandicoot; it woke me out of my dream. My hands clenched the steering wheel, using it as a lever to get a better look over the dashboard. Straining my eyes for something, anything. Couldn't see much past the sign but murky shifting shadows, nothing to be scared about. Not that I wanted to get out. Wait, there it is again, the flash of something shiny just to the left of the signpost. I could see it clearly. I was mesmerised, it was beautiful. I buttoned up my jacket and slowly stepped out of the car, not even blinking for fear of it disappearing again. Is this what I was brought here for? Is this where it wants me to be?...

Could it really be? I came a little closer, curious to get a better look. The funny thing was, that the nearer I got, the farther away it seemed to be. I'd take a step towards it and it seemed to move back. Deeper into the forest I went, playing follow-the-leader. Until, finally I came to a clearing. The air was still and I was oblivious to anything around me but the scene which unfolded before me... It was like I was dreaming, a hazy silver light swirling in the darkness of the forest, surrounding me, gently filling me up with its fragrance of sweet perfume. I could feel it caressing me and then it appeared to pull back momentarily. Like it was looking at me, a figure formed. A female figure approaching me from the mist, as she got closer I recognised her at once. It was MJ. She smiled and took my hand. I eagerly accepted it, my mind was racing. I didn't understand.

"You disappeared, where have you been?... I've never been able to let go of you, I loved you so much." Smiling, she drew me into the mist and kissed me. It was as if no time had passed, holding me in her arms... It was so real.

"I've been waiting for you, Collin."

"Here... In the forest?"

"In a way yes, for this is the only place you can reach the Silver City, although for me it was like it was yesterday. Time stands still here."

"But we looked everywhere for you. We thought you were dead. My mind searched for some kind of explanation. You mean you were here all the time?"

"Yes... I was, I could still come back now if I chose, but I have found my true home," Come with me, Collin." MJ looked into my eyes and I suddenly felt calm, like we were one.

Leading me back the way we came, everything around me, the vegetation, the wildlife, was like liquid silver and as we walked away, I turned back and looked towards the clearing in the woods. I could see the doorway from where we entered into this strange world, a hazy yet dull green hole.

My ute was still where I parked it... but it was kind of different now. The car had an energy of its own, in my mind I could feel it welcoming me. I followed MJ in.

"Where are we going?"

"Down the highway of eternity," she whispered.

"Who are you really?... Tell me."

"I am the wind."

I reached for her hand... feeling drunk with the same love I felt for her back when we were kids, I held her tight, started the engine and drove off into the night... giggling like the night we went out on our first date.

DRIVING HOME DRUNKS

By Gregory Bogaerts

What's the matter driver?!
Yeah, what's the matta with yer?! Why aren't ya happy?!
We're happy!! Both of us!!
Yeah, we've hadda great night! Started drinkin' yesterd'y aft'noon!
Yeah. Great! So what's wrong! Eh!! You'd 'ave t'be a queer c**t not t'be enjoyin' yerself!!
What's that! You've been drivin' for twelve hours!!
Christ!! I'm glad it's a short trip!!
Yeah, if we'd known yu'd been drivin' for that long we'd 'ave got anotha cab!
Yeah, we would 'ave!
You hungry bastards ain't got no shame! I mean 'ave ya?'! Workin' those hours!
Yeah, could 'ave an accident!
Yeah, kill someone!
What? Waddya say? Us hopefully? Don't be smart driver!! We're payin'. We'll tell the jokes!!
Yeah, we don't need no smartarse taxi driver doin' one liners!!
And shithouse ones at that!
Yeah. Shithouse ones at that!
So why arncha happy, driver?!
Go on! Speak up!! What? Another three twelve-hour shifts this week?! Well, why work it?! Yer could be out on the piss like Darren and me!
Yeah, why work it? What? T'feed the wife and kids! Shit Yer not married are yer driver?!

What?! Yer are?! Christ no wonder yer drive cabs!!
Marriage's for mugs! So's cab drivin' by the look of yer, yer
miserable bastard!!

We want yer t'be happy driver!!

Yeah, in fact we insist on it!!

Know what we mean?! Driver!! We don't like bein' driven
home by some miserable c**t like you!!

Yeah. Miserable morose c**t!

So smile when we tell yer to!!

Yeah, it won't hurt yer! Probably scare the shit outta ya if
yer look in the rear-vision!

What's that?! Speak up!!

Don't mutter!!

Yeah. What's that noise?

It's his teeth!

What?!

It's his teeth! Grindin'.!

Well, stop it driver! It's getting' on me nerves!! Worse than
fingernails down a blackboard!

Christ! Didya have t'say that?!

Sorry! Don't pick on me! Take it out on the driver!! That's
what he gets paid for! Isn't it, driver?! What? Yer get paid
t'take us home?!

Ha! ha! Funny, driver. That's what you think.

Yeah, that's what you think!

Me mum 'ud say you 'ad another thing comin'! What?
Waddya say? No one like me could have a mother!! Listen
driver, I don't think yer goin' t'last the journey!!

No, that's right!!

Yeah, look at yer. Yer no oil paintin'!

Yeah, ugly as a monkey's arsehole!!

Yeah!! A hundred monkeys' ars'oles!

What d'ya say driver?! Rangatangs are better behaved than us!!
Waddya mean?! We're behavin' ourselves!!
Yeah, this's nothin' compared t'the stick we give some cabbies!
Yeah, yer should be grateful we're goin' easy on yer driver!
Yeah, we're even concerned about yer! Why yer aren't happy.
We're worried.
Yeah. Real worried!
We aren't yer drunken yobbos!!
Nah! Not us! We're SNAPS!
SNAPS?!
Sensitive New Age Passengers.
Yeah, yeah. That's right. Sensitive New Age Passengers.
What?! Waddya say driver?! Senseless New Age Pricks!!!
Listen yer bastard, yer really pushin' yer luck!!
Yeah, if we could stand up we'd give yer a beltin' yer'd never forget!!
Yeah! Beltin' yer'd never forget!
It's miserable bastards like you, driver, that make this world a shitty place t'live in.
Yeah. Shitty place! Horrible!!
Why d'yer think we drink?!
Yeah, we drink because the world's a shitty place with ugly morose and miserable bastards like you!!
Yer don't realise how lucky yer are driver! Drivin' round makin' money! Pickin' up nice blokes like me and Darren who just wanna chat.
And what do we get in return?! Insults!! Told we can't behave!
Waddya say driver? We'd only behave if we were asleep or dead?!
Listen driver, I've just about had enough of yer! I've got a good mind t'take yer number and report yer t'the Co-op!
Yeah, yer number. Then you'd be in the shit!
Yeah, you and y'missus and the kids 'ud starve!

Yeah, we could do that t'yer driver! Get yer licence taken away from yer!

Yeah, all 'cause yer can't keep a civil tongue in yer head! What? Waddya say now?! We haven't got a brain in our heads?!

Listen smart-arse! I passed the School Certificate English and Darren here passed the Maths.

Yeah, I got the Maths! Between us we aced the School Certificate!! Meat for the takin'!

Yeah, so don't get snotty with us, driver!

No, yer conceited mongrel!!

What's conceited mean?

Up 'imself!!

Oh yeah. Yer so far up yerself driver you'd 'ave t'fart t'blow yer nose!

Yeah! Ha! Ha! Wonder 'e's ever seen daylight!

Ooh geez, I don't feel so good!

What's wrong?!

Must been those two burgers I ate at the all-nighters. On top of the twelve schooners.

I told yer not t'eat that bastard's burgers! He uses horsemeat and cat!

Bullshit!!

He does! You'll wake up t'morrow sittin' on that palin' fence up the backyard. Howlin'!

Shut up Darren!! Yer not funny! I feel horrible! I think I'm gonna spew!!

What's wrong driver? He only feels crook! Why 'ave yer gone all white for? Waddya mean its fifty bucks if he spews in yer cab?!

Yeah, I can spew in it if I want to! I'm payin' the fare! It's a free country, ain't it?!

Yeah, a free country!

What? You'll pull over if I wanna throw up. All right. Just t'make yer happy, driver. If I spew in the gutter it might put a smile on yer face.

I reckon it's the driver's drivin' that's done it!

Yeah, yer might be right Darren.

I am right!! Shit, it's like bein' on one of them big Greyhound buses every time 'e hits the brakes. Like bein' outside off Nobby's fishin' in a big swell!

Ooh Christ!! Don't say that, Darren. Pull over quick, driver!!

Just hang five, driver! I'll just hold him by the collar out the door. Yeah, go on. Have a cigarette t'calm yer nerves while he's getting' rid of those burgers. That's a shockin' sight. All that Toohey's and cat meat mixed together.

Darren! Shut up!!

Don't talk! You'll choke on the vomit.

I think I've finished.

I reckon yer have. Isn't that yer heart and lungs in the gutter there?! Jesus, yer almost as pale as the driver. Don't worry driver he only got a bit on the back wheel and a few chunks on the floor. Yeah, I know it smells shockin'. What? The spray can. Yeah, yer might be right. Jesus, it's strong that deodoriser. Does the trick. Oh, hold on. It's upset his guts. Yep, he's gonna bark again! Just relax, driver. There can't be much left.

Oh, that's better. Thanks Darren.

Yer don't look better. Yer look dreadful!.

I'm finished. Hey, did the driver leave that meter tickin' while I was havin'a Ralph?!

I think the bastard did!

Darren and me aren't payin' yer for the time I spent havin'a spew!

Yeah, yer shoulda turned off the meter. What? Waddya say? Chuckin' up's classified as waitin' time?!

Waitin' for what?!

Yeah, waitin' for what!? Waddya mean yer time's valuable?! Yer only a shit for brains cabbie!!

Yeah, ten cents a dozen! Not even worth ten cents.

Yeah, drive on Cabbie!! We'll take a dollar off the fare when we get there!

Yeah. More than a dollar? That was a two-dollar chuck any day!! Who d'ya think'll win t'morrow Darren? The Knights?

Y'mean t'day. It's Sunday y'know. 5.00am.

Oh yeah. Shit! Already?! The sun's comin' up! I can't believe it! We couldn't 'ave stayed out all this time!!

We have. The Knights'll win!

Yeah! They'll flog Canberra!! The green slime machine 'ull come unstuck!

Yeah! Our boys'll stick it right up 'em! The pack'll hit em like a ton of bricks!! Daley and Stewart won't know what hit 'em!!

Yeah! That's right!!

D'ya follow the Knights, driver?! What?!!!! Y'don't?!! Y'don't follow football at all???!

Well, Christ, waddya do?? You'd 'ave t' be a queer c**t not t'follow football!! Waddya do??!

What? Yer go bush walkin'!!!

Christ almighty, the only greenie cabbie in Newcastle and we get lumbered with 'im!!

Why would ya wanna go bush walkin' when yer can come and see the Knights in yer own back yard?! No sense of floggin' round the rubbity dub getting' leeches on yer and stung t'buggery by ants and mozzies! What?? Yer like t'get away from Newcastle?! Why?! This's God's own country!!

Yeah, why don't yer like Newcastle, driver?! Sun and sand and vineyards and drink and women!! And most of all a great football team! What? Yer didn't say that yer hated Newcastle! Well it sounds like it don't it, Darren?!

Yeah! It does!! D'ya think yer too good for Newcastle, driver?

Yeah, if yer too good why doncha leave?!

Yeah! Em...em...migrate!!

To the South Pole yer whingin' bastard!!

Yeah, you're a whingin' bastard driver! Yer not a pommie are yer, driver?! Yer sound a bit posh!!

Sounds like 'e's got a carrot stuck up his bum, Darren!

Yeah, a carrot! Is that what makes yer talk so funny, driver?!

Yeah, yer strange, driver. Fancy goin' bush walkin'! Waddya say?! Y'don't like the violence on the football field?!!

What?!! There's no violence!!! Waddya talkin' about, driver??!

Yeah, there's no violence! Shit, yer stupid c**t! What's a few facial massages and a nice crisp uppercut in a scrum?!

Just love-taps. Part of the game. Not really violence!! What? Y'don't want yer kids t'see it?!

Wadya mean?! It'd do 'em good. Good dose of League! Should take 'em along, driver. Get 'em t'start playin' in the junior grades. Work their way up. Make a packet!

Yeah, yer wouldn't 'ave t'drive these, driver. Yer kids could look after yer in yer old age. Eh, driver?! Eh!! Waddya reckon?!

Hey, Darren check out th' sheila in the black stockin's at the lights.

Yeah, nice legs!!

'Magine those wrap't round yer head!!

Yeah. We'd give her one!

Yeah.

What's wrong, driver?! Waddya shakin' yer head for?!

Yeah and laughin'!! Waddya mean we couldn't raise a smile let alone anything else?!

Yeah! Waddya mean?! We'd be able t'give it to her!!

Yeah, like those blokes at Stockton that gave it to that sheila!!

Yeah, well and truly!

What? Waddya say?! They should be in jail?!

Why?!

Yeah why?? What!! Rape and murder?!

Come off it, yer queer c**t!! She was askin' for it!!!

Yeah! Every one knew she was the town bike!!

Yeah! Got what she deserved!! The slut!!

Yeah, a slut!!

Reckon they pissed on 'er! Too good for 'er, I reckon!

Yeah! And 'er parents! Whingin' bastards like you, driver!! Reckoned they'd been victimised?! Phone calls? Waddya 'xpect with a mole for a daughter?!!

Yeah, only getting' what they deserve!!

Hey!! Driver!! Waddya stoppin' for?! What?! Yer want us out?!! Why?!!

We're not home!! What?! Get out and walk?!

You're a f**kin' c**t, driver!! We're takin' yer number!!

Yeah, the Co-op'll hear about this! Puttin' us out for no reason!!

Yeah, and you be real careful driver! We know you now!

Yeah, we'll spread the word! We've got plenty of mates! They'll be on the lookout!!

Get f**ked, driver!!

Yeah, get f**ked!!

FACE VALUE

By J. A. Kent

He was on schedule so far, when he stopped for breakfast, but Brisbane remained an eternity away and he was tired.

And it wasn't because he wasn't legal. He wasn't one of those truckies who popped pep pills and faked logbooks to meet impossible schedules. He had stopped to sleep the previous night at a roadside parking place. Only the truck that had parked behind him was loaded with cattle and their discontented stamping and bellowing throughout the night disturbed his rest.

Bloody stupid cows!

After breakfasting and before resuming his journey, he walked around the truck, automatically examining tyres, lights and reflectors – checking the load and its ties, the various connections between prime mover and trailer and insect kill on the windscreen.

"Any chance of a lift, Mister?" The unexpected voice startled him.

Young, clean-cut   well dressed, not the usual dole-bludger type heading north for the winter and always pestering for a lift. A backpack, slung over one shoulder.

Normally he avoided hitchhikers. Truck drivers had been beaten up and robbed by people they had picked up.

About twenty-five – older than the usual run of hitchhikers thumbing their way north during the autumn months. Nothing wrong with this fellow. And company might help him stay awake.

"Sure," he said, "if you're heading north. Climb aboard."

"Thanks," the young man said, smiling pleasantly...

Not many kids know to say thanks.

His passenger clambered into the cabin and fastened his seat belt without being told. He remained silent as the driver started the truck and manoeuvered towards the busy highway. The backpack rested on the floor, between his legs.

"What's your name, fella?"

"Michael."

The driver laughed. "I bet you get Mick?"

"Most of the time. My aunt hated it."

"Are you heading north looking for work?"

His passenger laughed. "In Queensland when it's coming winter and it's frosty down south?" He shook his head. "No, I'm just getting away for a while, a bit of a break."

Sensible kid. At this time of the year the Queensland job queues are filled with southerners looking for work. But then the bludgers don't want to work and know that they won't be hired. They had to make a show of looking for work though, if they are to continue receiving the dole.

Bludgers!

"Holidays, aye?"

"Yes."

"No ties, you're not married?"

The passenger stared through the side window. "No, but I was engaged once." He shrugged. "It didn't work."

"Sorry – "

Don't ask too many awkward questions, Jack. Get too personal and the youngster'll clam up. You need his conversation to keep you awake.

"How far do you plan on going?"

Michael shrugged. "Cairns perhaps, depends on how easy it is to thumb rides."

The driver glanced at his passenger curiously. "I would have thought it easier by bus?"

"Have you ever travelled on an interstater? The younger man laughed and shook his head. "Their objective is to get from point A to point B running to an impossible schedule. They stop every three or so hours at seedy roadhouses where everyone is made to get off the bus and the food, once you've queued for it, is greasy and cold. There's rarely decent showers or toilet facilities. No thanks; one bus trip is enough to last a lifetime. At least when you're hitching you can stop when and where you want. You truckies though, don't seem all that keen on hitchhikers."

The driver nodded. "There's been a few nasty incidents recently, two bashings that I know of and a rig hijacked."

"Stupid damned kids or organised crims?" His passenger shrugged. "Whatever they are, the bloody idiots have made it tough for fair dinkum hitchhikers."

Fair Dinkum! That good old Australian expression you don't hear from young people, not nowadays. He was fair dinkum himself, this one, no screwed-up dole bludger.

"Holidays – then you have a regular job?"

"Yes." His passenger nodded. "I'm a financial consultant. I tell people what to do with their money."

The driver laughed. "Those who have money! You wouldn't have much success with truckies like me. You have family?"

"No, my folks passed on when I was a nipper and I was raised by my aunt. She's gone too, now."

"Sorry – so where do you hail from?"

"Blacktown. I have a bed-sitter there. It's quite nice, close to work. Lonely at times, though."

A bed-sitter! Bloody hell! His was a lonely enough life, but at least he had a wife waiting for him at home and the grandkids called often. But to go home to a bed-sitter with nothing but a television and four walls and no one to talk to – bloody hell!

59

"Sometimes a single man's bed-sitter sounds attractive," he said. "When I get home there's a lawnmower for me." He laughed. "Glad of your company now though, Mick – yappin' keeps me awake."

"You've been driving all night?" Michael seemed concerned.

"No, I'm no bloody fool! I've got no desire for an early ticket to truckie's heaven, or hell, whatever it might be."

He told his passenger about the cattle that disturbed his sleep.

"You follow the footie?" the driver asked later.

"Since I was knee-high to a grasshopper." Michael's face lit up with passion. "My aunt was mad keen. She never missed a match, in fact wanted me to be a professional footballer. But I didn't even make the high school team. I took up pistol shooting instead. She thought that was for wimps and told me I'd never make a dollar with a pistol." He laughed quietly, almost to himself. "Still, her love for the game rubbed off, I reckon and I've been a St George fan for – forever."

"You picked the right team." The driver nodded emphatically. "I'm for the Dragons myself." They were on common ground and the young man was not only an avid fan but knew more about the team and its history than he did and he'd been a St George fan for a lot more years than his companion. The hours and kilometres passed quickly as they discussed and debated matches and results.

Good god! He had forgotten how weary he had been. This kid knows what he's talking about but by the same token he's willing to listen. Good kid, this one – every driver would be better off with a Michael as a passenger, during long interstate hauls.

They stopped for lunch at a roadhouse, the driver paying. "Worth it," he said. "You've made the trip easier for me. Watch for me on your way home, I run this route often. You'll be right on for a lift with me."

"I will," Michael promised, shouldering the backpack. Although the driver had suggested that he leave it in the truck while they ate, he had still brought it with him.

"Next stop Brisbane," the driver said. "And once across the Tweed it's rough going."

He swore as he eased the big vehicle into the increasing stream of traffic. "Bloody rubber-neckers. They don't know their right from their left and have never heard of turn indicators!"

"I'm surprised you drive this route, I thought most truckies favoured the New England Highway?"

"Most do, but my bread and butter is the coast road. There's regular haulage for me all the way up and down the seaboard. I'm hauling a load from Newcastle now and there'll be groceries for Grafton on my way back and produce from Grafton to The Smoke." He grinned at his passenger. "You're right lad, it's easier truckin' up and down The New England, but the coast road's kept the wolf from my door for a lot of years."

Michael grunted. "I don't think it'd be my cup of tea, though," he said. "I doubt if I could stand the same old scene day after day."

"Life in the fast lane, aye, you financial advisers? But to each his own, Mick. I'd go bananas in a week in your city office. You're happy telling people what they can do with their money and I'm happy drivin' my rig. But at least we agree on footie teams. You got a place to stay in Brisbane?"

His passenger was leaning forward, watching the road ahead. "I don't want to go into Brisbane," he said.

"I was about to ask you to drop me off at the bypass."

Disappointed? Good heavens – because the youngster didn't want to travel into Brisbane with him? Good company, the kid, interesting to talk to, polite, well- mannered, clean-cut too. Not one of the usual type, those with the long hair and half beards and earrings, the dirty jeans, faded T-shirts and tales of woe one pretended to believe but didn't. No dole bludger, this kid. Just a young man taking a different holiday, adventuring perhaps, taking a few risks. Good on him, he had a lot that most youngsters lacked nowadays, sadly.

Yeah, he was disappointed. He'd miss his company.

"No problem," he answered casually. "At least you won't have to put up with my bad language when I strike the city traffic. But you might find it difficult to hitch a lift on the bypass; best I drop you off at the servo ahead. It's a truckie stop and you're bound to strike someone heading north."

"That's good of you."

Clutching his backpack, the young man opened the door as the truck eased to a stop in front of the service station. "Thanks for the ride."

"No worries." He hesitated then held out his hand. "The name's Jack, Mick, perhaps I'll see you at the footie sometime?"

The handshake was brief. "Thanks, I'll look forward to it."

"Any rate, watch out for me when you're heading back south…"

"Sure." And then he was gone and the driver watched him walking across the cement drive-in area towards a number of parked trucks. The young man didn't look back.

Disappointed – Yes, he was disappointed.

He shrugged.

Ships in the night, isn't that what they said – ships in the night?

He hauled into the suburban freight yard a half-hour ahead of schedule and was pleased to find a load waiting for the return trip.

"Great," he said to Markham, the dispatcher. "I'll be moving out around four." He hoisted his overnight bag from the vehicle's cab. "There's room at the pub?"

"There's always a room for you there, Jack."

"Good oh!" A decent feed, a shower and a few hours sleep and he'd be right for the road again.

"By the way, Jack," Markham said, flicking through the papers on his clipboard before removing a facsimile sheet.

"I don't suppose you've seen his bloke?"

It wasn't a good photograph, photocopies rarely are, but it was clear enough for Jack to recognise his recent passenger. "Who is he?"

"Some bloke named West, Michael West, armed robber, he is…"

"I tell people what to do with their money –"

THE SMELL OF BITUMEN

By Nerida Melsmith

The first rain of autumn falls hard, pummels me. Spurts of dust, tiny tendrils of breath from each drop of water, a slight hiss as the cold hits my back. I am a modern song line. I can go forever, with grand names. But in truth I am a multitude of different textures, each with a differing surface feel. Some tyres grab me, others glide softly, most race over me, others inch forward even when stationary.

Hot sun warms my back, soaks into my layers. The bitumen holding the gravel relaxes, spreading into the gaps. On heat wave days it melts slightly and the stones nestle down lower to avoid the burn. Soft feet get speckles of black stuck to them, like a feather they dash across me. Usually on the way to the beach, having forgotten the thongs, the legs jump up and down from one foot to the other. They stand on one leg, trying to maintain balance as they keep the foot on the thin line of shadow the pole casts on edge of the beach-path.

Footpath and I have an uneasy peace, especially when they cut into my sprawling edges and dig trenches, narrowing my surface. The smooth whish over my back becomes stops and starts, the impatience transmitting down from the driver's wheel through the four wheels to me. They dig down to the underside, through the soil, the rocks, to expose clay. The men shovel and dig and smooth and create a surface, ready for the topping of sand, then the gravel, and then the roller comes back and flattens it. It gets busy with cars and trucks lining up, blocking the side streets. At the same time, the men settle on their shovels as they prepare for the next step, the bitumen. The yellow machine, half the width of the road, towers over the men.

It snorts and hisses and blows steam, and at the back a band of pipes dribbles black rain on the gravel. It moves slowly, evenly, and with authority; the man steering, a miniature figure high in the cabin.

The smell of bitumen, strong and fresh, fills the air and brings the neighbours out to watch. A formwork of planks and mesh delineates the boundary. Green trucks drive up and their long elephant trunks spill grey wet slug along the form. The cylinder turns in a continual circular movement. The slug flops against the barrel sides, flicking bits into the cavern and onto passing cars. Men walk alongside leading the trunk. A man watches and walks where he can, calls to the driver, "Slower!" as he guides truck and its grey load of concrete. Another throws spills of slug back into the formwork. At the rear, the metal scraper moves slowly turning the wet mass into angles and gutter shapes. Then the laughing team come with their trowels and flatteners and quickly smooth the top. They are on alert, running back and forth, checking the surface.

The labrador sniffs, putting a paw in, testing – cold and wet, so withdraws. The dog stands and watches the man run back and look at his print before smoothing it with his trowel. He reaches out and ruffles the dog's neck. "Go on with you. Get!" He bangs his fist on the trowel, frightening the dog off. Not like the indoor dog, from thirty-five stories up, down for the daily walk, with soft pads from shiny floorboards and wool carpet, suffering as stones graze the pads. The dog dances in quick steps, mystifying his owner.

They trip; coming out to get their paper. He with his silver stick, she holding his arm, clutching her cardigan, hesitating at the curb, stepping down and hurrying as the pedestrian beeping ceases. Thin translucent skin gives way as she stumbles over her feet, her hand brushing my surface. My rough top catches and holds her, not quick enough to differentiate between rubber and skin. The shreds stick. Her hand bleeds. She shakes. He can't pull her up without coming down. The wail of the siren becomes louder. The two uniforms help her up and take her to the curb. A motorist stopped by the bundle on the road, turns the old man around and leads him over to her. Honking cars swerve to avoid the flashing blue lights. Order is restored. The antiseptic cream and the dressing protect the frail skin. She can't use her hand. She refuses hospital. The police drive them home. His paper rolled against the new curb. I know it will disintegrate before he remembers to collect it.

Underneath I feel the soft scrap, a worm. Not so often now as it is winter. The warmth from the tyre friction and the weak sun heats my back. Pockets of air form and myriads of insects create temporary homes and resting places in their travels. Tiny paws scratch and rub as my underside is rough and uneven, resting on gravel, which rests on sand. The young mice like to get up close to the under-surface. They squeeze themselves between the bituminised stones. I hear tiny squeaks and yelps as vibrations shakes their tiny bodies.

Never any bigger bodies come this close. It is dangerous. A continual load above, heavy rain after a dry spell and I crack. There have been several drownings as it takes the next truck to pressurise the mesh of stones to lose their grip in bitumen and part. The squeaking and flurrying was a shock to me. I realised these young ones were defying their parents and seeking out thrills.

The air spaces were filled with dried grass, bits of paper and effectively barred off. I missed their play.

A collapse is painful for me as the tyre goes down; the driver will accelerate and spin his wheel out, drag the bottom edge of his car and sear along my surface leaving a scar. Other cars will avoid the hole. There will be much honking and swerving and the crunch of metal scraping metal in the distance, a siren and the uniforms. Such change, the tyres slow down. Voices quieten and men in yellow hats arrive in a truck filled with equipment. They pull off orange cones and place them around the hole. They get tall poles and tie red and white striped ribbon around them and prevent the cars driving across the hole. One of the men squats down, feels the hole edge and tries to break a bit or kicks it with his boot. Underneath I feel small movement away from the light and noise.

Marcy will often surprise me and stick her nose out. Marcy moves around in lower world. Her pink grey feet with their flexible claws seem to grab on to anything, even smooth and slippery surfaces.

"Bloody rats," the voices say, "What with the water and the traffic counter increase, we now have rats tunnelling everywhere."

Not a week goes by without her dropping by to let me know of some happening. She'd go on listing family exploits like the Book of Genesis. It seems to me her lot have just had babies and the next thing they're having babies again, with hardly a breath in between. Marcy catches me up on the gossip up and down the sections. Her favourite haunts cover the shopping strip, past the hospital and, occasionally, to the river.

With all the fights and a bid from the water rats to secure more riverbank, not to mention the tragic poisoning case at the hospital, her clan has diminished to three thousand. With spring she is expecting a big increase. She watches out, checks if the babies aren't feeding and why families are moving to the surface and who is dying from eating bait. I call her The Godmother. No one messes with Marcy and she has the scars to prove it. She likes to sit in the erosion at the edge of the open drain.

She has created quite a respectable sitting space, pinching the mice's grasses, close enough to the under-surface to get the vibration, and hidden away from the grate and poking sticks and falling rubbish. Quite some distance below in the big drain, her cousins were being trapped, not the usual trap, but a fine invisible mesh and then grabbed by the tail and swung against the wall. It got worse she told me, so bad, word was travelling around the city to warn the younger ones who were being targeted. She was not one for rumour or sentiment, my Marcy, but she'd been told there was blood-letting and the river rats said they'd seen bones, clean and scraped, come out the drain outlet.

Food was getting harder to find on the surface. Restaurants were putting their scraps in "vermin proof" bins. Rubbish was being collected regularly. Charities were making fewer leftover pick-ups, where always a few loaves would fall off the rack. There are no predators down there. She'd heard a few juveniles saying watch out for boys. Not a place for humans. Marcy and I agreed on that. Dark smelly putrid water rose from ankle depth to five feet or more after rain. Marcy has seen one or two humans down there, not that she liked the drains much. It was an emergency after a flood and she knew the alternative route, which avoided the water. It was her first body, pudgy grey, a ghost floating on its long journey towards the bay.

But now she'd heard there were live bodies going down, not with ladders and lights and equipment gas masks. These had little clothing and torn sneakers, came through broken grates and manholes shouting and banging the tunnel walls with pipe lengths. She asked me to pass the message to road sections with grates.

I, in turn, told her about the body I had seen. Red and oozing, taken away, and later a young girl came and stroked the faded dark patch near the gutter.

She left yellow flowers. For several days cars moved evenly, the tyres smooth and even, no squealing and burning strips on my surface, as if in mourning.

It has been quiet. I glimpse two flashing lights at night and hear the roar of traffic high up, above the river. Those young ones, the fancy freeways, arch bigger, stand higher and want the cars faster. For them, the thrill of limitless, the longer camber, the harder curve. I snuggle down on to my under-surface and relax, comfortable to have fewer tyres, old friends, coming their regular route home. Nervous of the new fast highway.

DRIVEN MAD

By Kerrie Henry

"FEAR ME". It is a sticker on the rear window of a grubby green utility. She sits behind it at the traffic lights while it revs impatiently. Exhaust fumes curl blue from the shine of a chrome exhaust pipe too clean for the rest of the car. Slogans on car stickers always catch her eye. This one though, unleashes its anger across the back windscreen in letters large and white and ragged with fury.

The green utility rears when the lights change, charging into the intersection like a spooked stallion. She watches it streak forward, taillights flaring as it pulls up sharp behind other cars. It weaves through the traffic until another red light jerks it to a stop. She slides into the lane beside him to steal a peep at the driver – to see what man, or boy, shouts at the world with such solid volume from the mute transparency of a car window. Grubby peaked cap – backwards. Face grey with the dust of every building site he has ever worked on. Two day's stubble. The final traces of adolescence pockmark his skin. Greasy tendrils of black hair are dragged into a thin rat's tail that scuttles down his back. Though sealed car windows muffle a heavy drumbeat, techno' music still billows like an audible miasma around his car. It's not music so much she thinks, just nervy synthetic sound sawing away at the ears. His impatient fingers dance an edgy erratic rhythm on the steering wheel.

She fights an irresistible urge to provoke him somehow. Though in the prime of early manhood, she finds him so incredibly unattractive. Yet she tinkers with the idea of catching his gaze and sinking one eyelid into a slow, seductive wink. She, wearing too much twin set and too little make-up, grey-haired and softened by years, by pregnancy and childbearing, stunning his bravado and emasculating him with shocked horror. She grins at the ironical possibility of it all. His sightless glance brushes her and then, distracted by impatience, rushes away. Her age gives her anonymity. He looks at her without noticing. The lights change. He is gone.

She travels this road often from her own home to her parents place in the country. Boredom sends her looking for entertainment – distraction. She finds it often stuck on car rear windows. People tell her their politics, religion, passion. She discovers their hobbies, their demographic, even their pets. "Love is a German Shepherd". She finds out more about perfect strangers on this road than she does about her neighbours or the woman beside her at a dinner party. On a car window or bumper they reveal all. On this journey she meets people without meeting them, knows them without exchanging a word. She is admitted into the intimacy of family tragedy. "Don't send your organs to heaven, heaven knows we need them here." When one heartbeat made all the difference, someone stuck a sticker on a car. She looks across to the driver of a car whose window glitters with "Magic happens." Instead of a witch's hooked nose and a crystal ball spinning above the dashboard, there is just someone ordinary believing that life can be extraordinary.

Still the utility dodges and darts through the traffic ahead. Still she wanders her car into the lane beside him at intersections. The Tortoise and the Hare. She wonders how many more minutes he calculates will be his at the end of his frantic drive. How much more time for living will he have accumulated after his journey? Annoyed that he is bringing out the worst in her, she feels great satisfaction when at last she leaves him snarling in traffic at a red-lit intersection.

It is a homing instinct that draws her from the highway, away from green utes and bumper stickers towards her parents' place.

The country road is long and straight and as familiar as home itself. Her stiffened back now accepts the softened contours of the driver's seat. Almost there. The road slips by. Still her little son sleeps. With a relaxed sleeper's hold, though still somehow possessive, his dimpled hands are draped over a small cement garden gnome her parents have given him. It is gaudy with good cheer and he insists on taking it wherever he goes.

Aproned and spotted or flowered, her mother will be at the door waiting before the car is halfway along the once rigidly pine-lined driveway. Now it is a corridor of young native plants that sway and shimmer blue-grey informally along the track that brings her to the home of her childhood.

"Well hello my little man!" her mother will chime as her fat hands clumsy with impatience struggle with the seat belt buckle. She has an urgent need to cradle him – wrap him around her heart with the surprising strength of arms gone flaccid with age. Her mother's enthusiasm for her grandson will sweep all before its energy. There will be too many sticky treats, too much lemonade, too many laughed-at winked-over tantrums. There will be a toy box garish with a cache of novelties her mother has gathered like a nesting magpie – an old camera, sunglasses, a broken wind-up clock – pickings from the church jumble sale, the CWA street stall and the kindergarten fete. Her father will massage the gruff muscle from his voice. His face will become supple with affection. He will walk his little grandson patiently through the orchard, leaning to hear his telegraphic infant speech. And then, though all others must tread the sacred sod of the old man's vegetable garden with utter reverence, the child will be allowed to trample though its harvest and pick the ripening vegetables.

On either side of the road the paddocks spread golden and flat. The arthritic limbs of isolated eucalypt giants reach, twisted into the sky. Baled hay patterns the space all the way to the horizon like a three-dimensional checkerboard. Crows coal-black and sunshine-sheened hunch along the fences and occasionally take lumbered flight. She passes the makeshift memorial beside the road where a cross stands to attention above the blur of a pastel posy. The flowers are always fresh. They lean into the wind that prowls the paddocks and fiddles distractedly with the silver wrapping. "Kaitee McPherson," the cross laments, "Killed tragically in a car accident here on November 4th, 1992. Only the good die young."

She marvels at the faithful heart that after all these years still weeps over this place hallowed by splattered blood.

Who kneels in the isolated stubble of a country roadside and with trembling fingers dedicates another floral tribute to a memory? she wonders. She slows. As she always does. Then she senses him. The green ute.

He is there filling her rear-vision mirror like the fat face of a schoolyard bully thrust too far into personal space. He sways and swerves into the oncoming lane. Double lines warn him off. He nudges her car's moving shadow. Draws so close. Slows. Draws close again. He needles and wheedles. She stares too often into the rear-vision mirror as he drags her attention from the road ahead. She brakes to temper his insistence. His middle finger springs from a closed fist and he mouths obscenities at her through her mirror. She decides not to provoke him further, but steadfastly clings to the speed limit.

The moment that she decides to pull over and let him pass is snatched from her. He arcs into the oncoming lane to overtake. Her self-righteous outrage becomes a softer thing as relief seeps through her. He draws level with her and she slows, anxious to see the road ahead swallow him. She sneaks a timid look. Aggression drags his mouth into ugly shapes. He fills the moving space between them with fury. She shifts her gaze back to the road. "Just go," she urges inwardly, "Just go."

He is almost past her and still his glaring locks her into its rage like an attacking dog that will not release its jaws. He is almost past her. Now he must screw his face around to look over his shoulder. This is his error. This is that one pivotal moment when a split second brings worlds to colliding. His intent abuse and determined aggression steal his attention. He misjudges his distance. Mistimes his manoeuvre.

There is a slight bump as the rear of his car clips the front of hers. Rocking. Sliding. Crumpling metal. Uncontrolled acceleration. Chaos. The world passing at speed. There is a moment when she believes she has retrieved power. Yes. She has control. Then everything is slipping away. There is no control, only moments, spinning into slow motion. Hundreds of thoughts distort catastrophe's time. Seconds seem to become minutes. She thinks not of herself but her sleeping baby.

When her place within a cataclysm stops spinning and fragmenting and only the dust is left flying, she knows. In the silence made extreme by the fury that preceded it, she knows. With heavy foreboding wringing her gut she slowly levers open her crumpled door, walks to the rear door, opens it and unbuckles her dead baby's seat belt. She sits with his body held against her own as if somehow she could squeeze her life into his. She hears a low animal wailing. It is a haunted haunting noise rising and falling. If death could sing this would be its tune. On, on it goes through the unmoved hay-baled paddocks. Out into the never-never. It is she who sings. Time passes.

A crow bleats. She lays her son tenderly on the grass and wanders. She sees "Fear Me" lying among scattered wreckage along the roadside where it has been thrown as if by a maelstrom. He whimpers. She leans towards him.

"Are you all right?" she asks. Her voice comes back to her from a long way off. "What can I do to help you?"

"You'd be a stupid f**king bitch," he says. Spit flecks his chin. "Look at me bloody car." In the ruin that surrounds them there is a bright thing, solid and heavy as a brick. Then it is in her hand and her arm is swinging wildly. His face is surprise, rippled with panic.

"And you," she says "You'd be a stupid bastard."

She drops the garden gnome and trudges back to where her baby lies. She gathers him into herself once more and sits. She bends her knees and wraps him around her chest, supporting him there with crooked legs. "No," she says. "No." And then the word gathers its own momentum and falls from her mouth in a stream that will flow until she herself has no breath. She rocks back and forward, back and forward, like a pendulum trying to wrench back time. To undo its tyranny. To rewind tragedy.

When help arrives it is a young woman. The chaos pales her, shrinks her. She wanders through the debris as though lost. Shock locks her hands to her mouth and then nervously they plough her hair. "My God." She repeats it over and over again. It is a mantra to fill her mind so there will be no space left for the vivid ugliness of what she sees. But when she comes to the woman, she sits beside her. Compassion instructs her to say nothing. It is only when she places an arm around the woman's shoulder she realises.

"Your baby…"she says. "My God." This time it is a prayer.

"What's his name?" she asks gently. The woman answers, then they sit in a wordless agonised place. Eventually the young woman speaks again.

"The other driver is dead. Did you know?"

The woman nods. More sodden moments slip by. She laughs at something unseen and then surrenders to the madness. Grief and its tears blur her world into surrealism.

"You're freezing. There's a blanket in my car," says the young woman. She leaves the woman and walks to her car. There is a sticker on the rear window. "Zero to bitch in ten seconds."

Less than half an hour ago the mother would have laughed. She does not laugh now. Will never laugh in quite the same way again.

SUMMER AT AUNT FLORRIE'S

By Laraine Day

"I'm watching you, Candy. Watching. You don't see me, but I see you."

The voice follows me. Even when it's silent, I know it's not far away. Like my shadow when the sun meets an obstacle. I'm used to the voice trailing when I stay here at my Aunt's place and would miss it if it stopped. It's a man's voice, not a harsh sound, no threat of the sinister. Sometimes there's a background rhythm: a whirring sound like the wheels of a truck on the highway.

The voice wakes me from my sleep. I lie in my bed, sheets securing me snugly with nurses' corners and through the darkness I look for the face that goes with the sound.

"I'm watching you, Candy."

I make a picture in my mind. I make the man's face young, without wrinkles, with hair, a rich dark mop of it. Give him all his own teeth, no gaps or stains. Nothing like my Uncle.

"Come along, Candy. Stop daydreaming. There'll be no fresh vegies at the market if we don't hurry." A female voice this time. Accompanied by a real face. That of Aunt Florrie.

"Sorry, Aunt Florrie," I say. I rush in tying my shoelaces, but there's a knack and for someone ten, a knack that haste will hinder.

"Here, let me," she says, one knee to the ground. Her fingers behave quickly and in order.

Once outside, I jog to stay in touch with her briskness. Despite her speed, I sense her shoulders – level with the brim of my straw hat – relax. Because Uncle Dirk is indoors.

He's dozing in the oversized swivel chair, awake only enough to follow the cricket on the television, in a room that reeks of whisky and inebriation. The sun shining over the test match, from the box in front of him, is all the summer he sees.

"Shut that curtain to," he says. "I'm being blinded".

"You should enjoy some sunshine, Uncle. Soon it'll be March – the nights will draw in and there'll be too much darkness."

"As I like it, child. As I like it."

He's more hungover than usual this morning. When I got up in the night to use the bathroom he was washing himself in the pan of the toilet. Vomit covered the porcelain hand basin, like a painting the artists call abstract. I had to feel my way to the outhouse at the end of the garden, while the voice kept guard.

"Let's check the list," my Aunt says, finding the scrap of paper at the bottom of her well-used shopping bag. "Chemist, bottle shop, vegies, then Griffin's."

I wonder why she writes a list, since the pattern is always the same. At the pharmacy we pick up Uncle Dirk's assortment. That's what I call it because I'm reminded of the pick 'n' mix in the milk bar. Green for heartburn, pink aspirins, orange painkillers for the gout. All in small genie jars. At the bottle shop we collect the medicine to wash them down.

To the market stall. Aunt Florrie chooses vegetables individually – each bean, every sprout. Fresh and firm to touch. At teatime she'll sauté and season, then savour, like a connoisseur with a vintage wine.

"Your Uncle always grew our vegies – prized ones too," she says. "See the garden now. A shambles. It's what the drink does, Candy."

I don't hear the voice when we're shopping, until we reach Griffin's Antique Shop. It hovers here, like a restless bird flapping between the branches of a tree, patrolling its young. Aunt Florrie and I mind the shop while Mr Griffin runs his errands and has his lunch.

"Are you sure, Florrie?" he asks. "I can put 'back in five' on the door."

"You go and eat your sandwich. Have an hour in the park," she tells him. I wonder if Mr Griffin knows that Aunt Florrie is glad of the excuse.

At the antique shop the same blanket of dust rises and resettles, trying to choke me on its journey. The shop is swollen with things of no value that Aunt Florrie calls collectables. But who would collect this stuff, apart from old Mrs Griffin before she keeled over and died?

Unwantables is what they really are. An accumulation of grimy leftovers. People leave battered old suitcases of paraphernalia in the doorways. Sometimes shiny new suitcases, eager to dispose of the junk inside.

I write a letter to my mother. Tell her how the summer holidays seem endless, but that I'm enjoying my stay with Aunt Florrie. Mum knows Uncle Dirk, so no need to pretend there.

It's best I'm here for the hols. Each weekend we go into the City to see the sights. Melbourne's so big and exciting. I hope you aren't working too hard. Miss you. Candy.

I don't mention the voice.

Eight weeks with no school. Aunt Florrie prides herself on her role as weekend tour guide: City Square where we dodge the seagulls flying like kamikaze planes; the majestic St Paul's where my Aunt peacefully rests her weary limbs, while my young legs scoot the aisles to marvel at mosaic and patterned glass. The voice comes with me.

"I love the cathedral, too, Candy."

On a trip along the Yarra the voice names each bridge for me as we pass underneath. I hear the chugging of a truck… or is it just the boat in harmony with my imagination?

"Princes Bridge…" the voice says softly.

"I know…"

"What's that, Candy?"

"Nothing, Aunt Florrie," I say. ''Thinking aloud."

"You should send a postcard to your mother, Candy," Aunt Florrie says at a souvenir kiosk.

I choose a glossy card with crinkly edges – a close-up shot of Flinders Street Station.

"Mum will like this," I say. "She told me once that the clock face is wide enough for a truck to drive around the outside. A truck as huge as the one my dad used to have."

I wonder if it's true or just one of those stories children get told for effect? The clock tower is tall and the face so high it's impossible to tell. Like trying to measure the moon.

When the clock strikes midday, twelve resounding booms fill my head, each of them counted out in a whisper by the voice.

"I sent Mum Parliament House last year," I say, pressing a licked stamp to the back of the card. "She keeps it on the mantelpiece and says she'll see it for herself one day."

"P'raps she thinks the Premier will be inviting her for tea." Aunt Florrie chuckles at her joke and her face looks its real age. Usually it looks older.

Every summer I stay with Aunt Florrie and Uncle Dirk.

"You go and enjoy Melbourne," Mum says. "Aunt Florrie has time to spend with you while I can work some extra shifts. Experience the City, Candy. There's more people queuing for an ice-cream in Bourke Street than you'll meet in this entire town."

In the antique shop Aunt Florrie creates a mist with the feather duster, while I read and look at pictures.

I blindly lift a heavy book and from behind it falls a small jar with tablets inside. The thick glass makes a clatter on the ground but doesn't smash. The contents are white, like peppermints.

"What have you done?" says Aunt Florrie. She doesn't mean to sound grumpy.

"They must belong to Mr Griffin," I say. I start to read the words stuck to the jar.

"Here. Give them to me," says my Aunt as if recognising the label.

I hear the voice then. "You're a good girl, Candy." It soothes and makes up for Aunt Florrie's impatience.

I sit cross-legged on the floor and read from an old book with a frayed spine. A layer of grime sits on the cover like a dusting of icing sugar on a sponge cake. The book has pictures of Melbourne's parks and gardens and I list the ones I'll ask Aunt Florrie to take me to.

She busies herself with the duster, piercing the loitering cobwebs, her left hand still clinging to the pills.

When Mr Griffin returns from his hour of sunshine, Aunt Florrie and I take a handle each of the shopping bag ready for the walk home. The return journey is slower than my Aunt's escape pace.

"Can we go to the Botanical Gardens this weekend? Feed the swans?"

"You take after your dad, Candy. He loved Melbourne. The gardens were his favourite."

I want to hear my Aunt talk about my dad. She rarely does and never in front of Uncle Dirk.

"He was special, Candy. Only twenty-five when he died. Your mum misses him, of course, but she had him in her life for only a short time. Your Uncle Dirk has twenty-five years of him to miss." I wait while Aunt Florrie gazes, harrowed by her memories. I will her to go on.

"We were devastated when he had the accident. We brought him up as a son, though he was Dirk's kid brother. As a boy all he ever wanted was to drive a truck. He had a toy truck that he took everywhere with him."

"And when he grew up he became a real truckie." I say it proudly.

Aunt Florrie's anguished brow makes her old and wrinkled and I think of an illustration in a Dickens story. Pain must age everyone, just as it did Miss Haversham.

"It killed him. Trucking. Killed your uncle too."

Aunt Florrie makes an effort to smile. "Sorry, Candy, I mustn't be like this. Yes, we'll go at the weekend. We'll take a picnic."

Friday is market day again. Aunt Florrie is preoccupied. She buys vegies but not the whisky and we don't call at the chemist. At the antique shop, instead of taking over from Mr Griffin, it's arranged for me to spend the afternoon with him.

I enjoy his company and try to like the dusty shop. Mr Griffin is the same age as Uncle Dirk but happier despite his bereavement.

I reach again for the big book and remember the tablets. "There were some pills," I say to Mr Griffin. "Oh, they were left from when Mrs Griffin was ill," he says. "They took her suffering away."

Mr Griffin gently takes my hand. "Have a closer look around the shop, Candy. See beyond the dust. Look into the heart of these objects. Things aren't always what they seem."

"Things aren't what they seem, Candy." It's the voice this time. "Look harder, Candy. Can you see me?"

I look into a mirror that balances itself on a bookshelf. The face I see inside isn't my own. It's the face that belongs to the voice. The face just as I had made it. The mop of hair, the smile and the kind, caring eyes.

"I can see you," I whisper. "Yes, I can see you."

The expression on the face changes to serious. Gives me a message.

"Watch and listen carefully, Candy. Go home now. Stop Aunt Florrie. Stop her from… Go now, Candy."

I hesitate only a second. No time to tell Mr Griffin. I run fast like the fieldsmen on the TV chasing the ball through the outer. I must beat it to the boundary.

I run harder and hear my step in tune with a siren.

Aunt Florrie wipes her hands on her apron. "What are you doing here, Candy?"

"It wasn't his fault, Aunt Florrie," I cry. "It wasn't Uncle Dirk. He didn't make my dad die."

"I know that, Candy." My Aunt looks desolate. "He's free of the pain now."

———————————————

I kick into the end of the bed, hating the way the corners tuck so rigid. Undercooked vegetables sit high on my insides not wanting to go down.

The voice settles me. "I'll look after him now, Candy," it says, and I hear a truck purring peacefully along a distant highway.

DAMAGES

By Tanya Wheeler

1

Wendy stopped her Gemini at a set of traffic lights. She gripped the steering wheel so tightly that her hands started to ache. Torrential rain hammered the cabin, sounding like machine-gun fire. She watched tiny hail bounce acrobatically off the bonnet. Squinting, she leant forward, her breath depositing a film of mist on the windscreen. She wiped the glass with the back of her hand, making the blurred lights of the city resemble iridescent paint bleeding on the dark easel of the night sky. The wipers whined along with the radio static that rendered the background music unidentifiable.

Wendy jumped as thunder shook the car. The surrounding suburb appeared like a black-and-white snapshot in the surreal luminance of the lightning flash. "Shit! That was close," she exclaimed, aware of the acrid odour of ozone penetrating the car's cabin. "What the hell am I doing here? I gotta be crazy. I can't see a thing. This'd be a damn sight easier if the bloody demister would work." She flicked the demister switch on and off, hoping to bully it into operating, then thumped the steering wheel. "You owe me big this time, Pete," she said out aloud to her absent husband.

2

Wendy was following her husband's work ute; white and non-descript like most work fleets. A sign advertising "A2Z Fabrications" in metallic azure on the driver's door was the only distinguishable feature. They were delivering the ute to Gerald, Pete's boss, for some renovations over the weekend.

"Why the hell couldn't you just swap cars with Gerald after work?" Wendy had asked her husband earlier. "Gerald could take the ute and you drive his Jag. Oh I forgot, you're not allowed to touch the Jaguar, sovereign-gold with genuine tan leather seats and six cup-holders, and we all know that you can tell a class vehicle by the number of cup-holders!" Wendy mimicked Gerald's bastardised accent of an expatriate Englishman. They had both laughed at Wendy's surprisingly accurate portrayal.

She had continued: "He really is a selfish pig. He expects me to follow you, at night, in my rust-bucket, to his country manor, God-knows-where in the sticks with a few hours' notice. It's not as if he lives just down the road. And you agreed without even asking me!"

"Honey, you know what Gerald's like," Pete had replied. "It's not easy to say no to him. Get the moody old bastard on a bad day and he's likely to sack someone just for looking at him the wrong way. Anyway, the ute's a company car. We'd be a hell of a lot worse off if Gerald took it away and he knows it. He wants the car this weekend and we just have to go and give it to him and that's that."

3

"Shit!" Wendy spat. "That's the third set of traffic lights he's gone through without waiting for me. Who the hell does he think he is? Schumacher? Not indicating, swapping lanes, running lights, speeding and in these conditions. How the hell does he expect me to keep up? How he's still got his licence, I don't know. What a lunatic behind the wheel. Yeah, and I'm one to talk. Don't they say that talking to yourself is the first sign of madness?"

Wendy slipped the clutch as she sped off the instant the traffic lights turned green. Scanning ahead, she spied the ute and followed it again through the suburbs to the outskirts of the city.

4

Gerald lived in a fashionable new estate adjoining a man-made lake that some developer with imaginative flair had named Lakeview Vista. It was one of those new satellite suburbs insidiously popping up like toadstools. A huge sign proclaiming Lakeview Vista's "rural lifestyle with city conveniences," guarded the estate's entrance under one of the few remaining eucalypts. The sign was accompanied by a diagram of the estate showing the future location of a primary school and a Woolworth's meant to be completed six months ago. The map was littered with "SOLD" stickers in red and white.

Pete parked the ute at the estate's entrance. "City conveniences but no damn street lighting." He directed the ute's high-beams at the map. "Figtree Way. There it is," he said after locating it on the diagram. "First right, then second cul-de-sac on the left."

Pete glanced in the rear-vision, seeing the trailing car a couple of hundred metres behind. He drove slowly. The car behind acknowledged him by flashing its lights, then Pete proceeded through the estate. The car following Pete continued along the main road, the self-righteous blare of its horn lost in the storm's cacophony.

5

Wendy braked too suddenly on a right-hand bend, locking the wheels and aquaplaning onto the shoulder. She held her breath, watching everything around her move in slow motion. Gradually, the car stopped sliding. She sat at the wheel, her hands shaking violently and her heart drumming louder than the rain on the roof. "Bastard!" she sobbed, watching the ute's taillights disappear up the road ahead.

Wendy closed her eyes and took deep, slow breaths. Rocking gently, she said, "I'm okay, over and over, like a mantra. Slowly, the sense of panic receded. She opened her eyes, feeling disoriented in the oppressive fog permeating the cabin from her breath. She unwound the window, grateful for the sobering effect of fresh air and rain.

Wendy had no idea where she was. It had taken all her concentration just to keep up with Pete, let alone focus on where they were heading. The ute had taken so many twists and turns that she had no notion in which direction to go. She decided to continue along the road, hoping to find a sign or something familiar.

6

"Oh my God!" Wendy shrieked when she saw the accident. The ute was wrapped around a tree. The headlights were still on, the beams directed at a sign saying, "Slippery When Wet". She started screaming uncontrollably as she raced through the deluge to the stricken vehicle. She tripped and fell onto her knees. "Please God, don't let him be dead," she prayed with her hands over her face.

Regaining her balance, Wendy wrenched off her muddy sandals and hurled them into the bush. Sobbing hysterically, she inched her way along the car to the passenger door. She tried to pry it open. "Open the goddamn door you son-of-a-bitch," she screamed as she slapped the window with her open palm.

Wendy grabbed a rock and hit the window. It fractured, leaving a spider-web pattern on the glass. She hit it again, shattering the web. She unlocked the door and climbed in. "You're going to be okay," she said trying to convince herself.

He was slumped over the steering wheel, silhouetted an eerie green from the dashboard lights. The radio continued playing, oblivious to the accident. The DJ was urging drivers to be extra cautious in the dangerous conditions.

The driver's window had imploded and the door smashed. It was replaced by the trunk of a large gum tree with a deep gash already oozing sap from the impact.

Wendy leaned over and felt for a pulse in his neck. Nothing. "Please God, no!" she wept. She checked his wrist, limp by his side. Still no pulse.

She put her face in her hands and howled, unconsciously rocking in time with AC/DC's Thunderstruck.

7

"Figtree Way. We're on the right track," Pete said, turning left into a cul-de-sac lined with topiary figs like giant lollipops. "Lot 14, that's it," the luminous numbers shining ghost-like. He pulled into the driveway and cut the engine.

"Where the hell is she?" Pete asked himself. He had been waiting for nearly ten minutes. "Surely she couldn't have missed the turn-off? She was just behind me."

Gerald's sensor light on the veranda flared again, revealing a fruit bat flying erratically in the sudden luminance.

"Shit! She is going to be so pissed," he said, drumming his fingers on the steering wheel.

Pete grabbed his mobile phone and dialled Wendy's number.

8

Wendy looked at the man beside her. She patted his dark hair affectionately with her hand, unaware of the ochre stain of blood on her palm. She leaned over and kissed his temple. Something smelt familiar, mixed with the acrid odour of blood. "You stupid son-of-a-bitch!" she spat, smelling the alcohol on him. "You're pissed!"

She felt the anger grow within her like the tempest outside. She grabbed his shoulders and threw him back in the seat. She gasped. Dark rivulets of blood stained the unfamiliar face. It wasn't Pete.

"Oh my God!" she choked, a wave of relief swamping her. "Thank you," she said with her head cradled in her hands, laughing and weeping all at once.

9

Wendy glared at the dead stranger. His mouth was agape like a sideshow clown. She leaned towards him and slapped his face as hard as she could, knocking his head into the damaged tree-trunk.

"You bastard!" She was shaking with rage. "That's for putting me through this. Nearly getting me killed, you drunkard son-of-a-bitch."

She grabbed his wallet from the console and spilt out its contents. She seized his licence. The snapshot of the smiling face looked nothing like the stranger beside her. She hurled it at the corpse. It fell face up on his leg, the picture smeared with blood. She tipped out his cash, a condom falling on her lap. She flicked it off in distaste like a soiled tissue. Eighty dollars in twenties. She pocketed it.

"Damages," she explained.

Wendy walked slowly back to her car. Her mobile phone ringing. She answered it, noticing that the rain had stopped.

DOWN THE RABBIT HOLE

By Julie Constable

"Have you ever fallen down a hole, Dr Mitchell?"

Dr Mitchell, a successful psychiatrist, was driving home. He worked in the city and lived in a large ranch-style house in a prestigious peninsular suburb. He often listened to the cassettes he made during his consultations, checking his first impressions, formulated while in close proximity to a patient, against a more detached position. He stopped the cassette. He found the woman's voice too seductive. She could even make falling down holes sound attractive.

He looked at himself in the rear-vision mirror of his red Saab. The cars banked up behind him. He smoothed out the frown line above his left eye and smiled at his handsome face. What a day. Two patients who allege they have fallen down holes. What is this? Hole week? The Year of the Hollow Earth? What about some alien abductions and severe probings?

A truck pulled up beside him in the turning lane, hissing like a dragon in the rain. Sometimes he had a good laugh on the drive home, making up for keeping cool during the sessions. But he didn't feel like laughing at Donna. Jim will restore some levity, he thought.

Rewind   Reverse play

"Hello Jim, I'm Dr Robert Mitchell..."

Fast Forward

He summarised Jim – a bespectacled, gangly, young man of 27. Low self-esteem... Lives in the country.

Play

"I took the colander. It was a new pink plastic one. The best blackberries grow along the creek at the bottom of the hill."
Dr Mitchell pictured Jim, the latent hunter-gathering streak warming his blood, his new pink plastic colander in hand, looking for bush tucker. The tall, yellowed grass of summer sends clouds of pollen into the air as he surveys the descent before him; his glasses glint in the sunlight. Donna called to him.

Reverse play

"... sometimes the hole chooses you..."
What a voice, he thought again. Her black hair was tousled like she had been gardening, falling down holes, or making love.

Reverse play

"I walked down the hill. Then I heard the pounding of my heart become louder and louder. I glanced over my shoulder and realised that the herd of steers was running full pelt behind me. I ran faster and faster towards the fence and grabbing the top wire threw myself over the top. I heard a scream and thought it was the pink colander or my glasses that had landed on the ground next to me..."
The doctor grinned. What is this? Patients giving themselves electric shocks. I could start up a new treatment – electric-fence therapy. Country weekend retreats. They probably do it for dares in the sticks. $5 if you piss on the fence, concrete head. Okay.

Fast forward

The car idled at another set of lights. The washers whacked the window, spreading the greasy rain from side to side.

Reverse play

"... I want to go back down there..."

Reverse play

"... go on Jim. What happened after you got up?"
"Well I walked towards the creek and I disturbed a rabbit grazing. It reacted strongly, leaping a good ten feet in the air and, on landing, disappeared. I'd never seen a rabbit do that before..."
The doctor missed the lights. He grew impatient. Come on, you bastards. Got to get through this time.
"Well, I started picking blackberries. Beauties they were. I wandered along the creek and came across a huge patch, the size of a shed. I walked around it, picking the berries and came across a tunnel on one side. I crawled in, being careful not to scratch myself. The tunnel opened out in the middle of the patch. It was a sort of clearing, you know, with the blackberries arching over the top. I could see the parent stems coming out of the earth as fat as my father's arm, thick and thorny..."
"How did you feel?"
"A bit funny. Sort of woozy. I felt there was all this energy pumping around me. Like when I went to Yallourn as a kid... Then the ground suddenly gave way beneath me."

Fast forward

The doctor had another thought. If I find some more patients with hole phobias and fetishes perhaps I could write a paper on it. Did they all read "Alice in Wonderland" as children? Yes, I'll blame it on the parents: "The Dangers of Reading Fantastic Fiction to Borderline Psychotics".

Play

"I kept falling. I thought it must have been a wombat hole, because it was too big for a rabbit hole. Then I thought that it wasn't really happening and that I'd passed out and I was lying on the grass dreaming. I thought if I could just reach out and feel the pink colander everything would be okay. But I didn't wake up. I kept falling. It was very dark. When I landed, I couldn't tell when my eyes were open or closed. I stared into the earth and after a while I could see little lights in the darkness. I thought: the earth has stars, too. I remembered I had a box of matches in my jeans and I pulled them out and struck one. Then I saw this blue, white sort of fibre on the sides of the tunnel. And two corridors branched out from this one horizontally. The stuff felt smooth and slightly sticky to touch. This is when I remembered something terrible...

Fast forward

Another red light. I hate this. I don't get home until after dark in winter.

Play

"Then I heard this sort of slithering noise and knew the Giant Worm was coming my way."

Stop

The rain eased and the sky turned indigo.

Reverse play

"It was so wonderful down there. I want to go back. No one understands."
"It's okay, don't cry."
"They think something's wrong with me. But you know I feel with the world the way it is, if you're not a bit crazy, there must be something wrong with you..."
"Do you have any recurring thoughts?"
"Well lately I've been trying to find this particular smell. As a child I had this book... I've been going to bookshops, libraries and op-shops, opening books searching for that smell. Waiting for that particular blend of glue, paper and ink to flood my brain."

Fast forward

"I've stopped reading newspapers. They make me cry."
The doctor recalled the way your mascara had run across your cheeks like the smudges of newspaper print...

Stop

Dr Mitchell entered the freeway and the traffic began to spread out. He thought the car sounded strange. The hum wasn't quite right. He accelerated and the hum changed pitch, progressing up the scales, blossoming into a hive of industrious bees at work. Okay, that's right. Except for the occasional cymbal crash. I might be imagining it. Or the car always sounds like this. Yes, that's it. I'm behind a blue Falcon. Sixty-five or sixty-six. The shoulders and back of the head of the driver give out no secrets. What was he thinking about? Me in the rear-vision mirror? KCC 056. Black-and-white number plate. Probably unroadworthy. Round tail-lights. My god! Think of something else … not you, Donna.

He hit the rewind by mistake.

Play

"I'll just get some background information from you. Age?"

Fast forward   Play

"Are you worried about money? Relationships?"

"My mother is paying for this or I wouldn't be here. You don't do this out of the goodness of your heart, do you? Gerald rang her…"

Fast forward   Play

"Tell me about the hole?"

"Well this hole appeared in the footpath. I was a bit scared, but I decided to jump in. You know how sometimes there are two voices inside you – one that keeps your feet standing on the edge of a cliff; and one that prompts you to fly. I wasn't sure if it was going to be a bottomless pit or what, but as I jumped I felt great. An orchestra played and it wasn't dark.

The hole levelled out and it was like fairytale land. A world beneath the world. I was flying through the air. Birds of all shapes and sizes flapped along beside me. Then I swam through the sea among thousands of brightly coloured fish.

Then I entered a tall forest. It was like a church. Closed in and coloured light falling in slivers and spots on the floor.

It was beautiful. Feeling and hearing the trees swish in the breeze. They talked to me in a watery language, which oozed upwards from the earth through their roots and was sounded by the leaves and wind. They bent and talked to each other. They made me want to cry. I realised my cheeks were wet with tears and that made me smile. It's hard to explain. Perhaps Nature only lets us see her uncovered for a moment. This time, she screened herself through my veil of tears…"

"Vale of tears?"

"V-e-i-l, though. You see."

She had looked beautiful at that point. I can see your face, Donna. Smiling in ecstasy.

"Do you know how close our DNA is to a tree's?"

Stop

Outside, the dusk spread and a whitish fungi grew over tops of the houses. Lights twinkled through the veil, like dew drops on a spider's web. Are they castanets clattering deep in the workings of the car? He visualised the car parked in the emergency lane, the bonnet open and himself staring at the car's innards with a thoughtful look on his face. Standing and listening to the hiss and click as the engine cools down. When you cried I wanted to take you in my arms. I stopped myself. I can't take a plunge, can I? He left the freeway. The dark country road became a tunnel in front of him.

Dr Mitchell saw something. A shadow on the road. A glint of eyeball. He applied the brakes. The car weaved to the left and scrunched on the gravel. Then came a soft collision. His airbag inflated and wrapped around the windscreen was a curtain of beautiful emerald filigree and blue circular designs. My God! I'm having a psychedelic accident! The car slid down the wet embankment into a fence. The car stopped. The cassette started.

"... I want to go back down there…"

The doctor felt strangely serene. His side window was missing and he didn't mind. What a beautiful evening. The air is fresh after the rain. And there's Venus on the western horizon. She glows silver, then gold; she seems to be expanding. Now red, redder and the disc grows smaller, concentrating the colour. Shrinking, shrinking… "… why can't I find the hole any more? What do I have to do?"

The doctor's reassuring tone spoke to him on the quiet road.

"I'll help you, Donna. It may take a little while, but we'll work through it…." Dr Mitchell tried the door handle; pulled back at the shock. After a few attempts he succeeded in opening the door. He crawled out of the car and lay down in the muddy grass.

"Have you ever fallen down a hole, Dr Mitchell?"

Venus returns. Bobbing up and down on the horizon. The earth must be wobbling…

"… the hole chooses you. I want someone to jump in with me…"

"It's so slippery!" he shouted over the crescendo of percussion his car was playing. "I'm falling, Donna."

Venus spread her iridescent fan, sparking the sky.

Please, a euphoric video fantastique and not the serpent tunnelling towards its prey…

Donna, are you there? I can hear singing. I can see stars behind my eyelids…

The peacock shook his head, readjusted his tail and jumped from the bonnet. He huffily high-stepped away from the accident. The electrified top wire of the fence twanged the roof of the car like a guitar string.

"… you would like to see what's down the hole, wouldn't you?"

NORTH COAST ROAD

By Ian Wynne

A low hill rises from the Durban North beachfront, its slopes a series of tree-lined roads and spacious homes surrounded by neatly-trimmed lawn.

It is quiet in the pre-dawn. A few lights flicker on, while on the beach one or two early walkers make their way along the sand. It is too early for most people to be stirring.

Behind the hill lies a valley of light industry. Along it runs the railway – and North Coast Road.

Ten kilometres inland the stillness has been gone for an hour or more, broken first by a starter motor grinding uselessly on a diseased engine, then by the sounds of a wakening community … ice-cold water pouring into a steel basin … cries of exhilaration as it is splashed over a naked torso … the dull mutter of a hundred thousand voices as the workforce rises.

In KwaMashu there is no time to linger in a warm bed. Soon the people are streaming from the mean concrete houses, smiles white against faces lost in the black of the night.

On the outskirts of the township the Putco buses stand ready, row upon row. One by one they fill with people. The throb of the idling engines fills the morning as first light comes to the sky.

Then, with an angry roar and a belch of black diesel, the workforce begins its journey to the city – via North Coast Road.

"I first saw the bus about six months ago," George Graham said, hunching forward in his chair. "I didn't really notice anything special about it at the time, except that it seemed bigger than the others. There was a massiveness about it that the others didn't seem to have."

The words ran into each other as the little man plucked nervously at his moustache. "I was driving along North Coast Road. I can't remember where I was going, but I remember how close the bus was behind me. They always do that you know; right up your backside so you haven't got a chance of stopping in a hurry without being shunted."

He paused for a moment. The brief torrent of words had emptied his lungs and he had to pant a little to fill them again. "It always makes me nervous, but that day it was worse. Normally I slow down, forcing them to overtake, or to slow down as well, but it was difficult. Every time I took my foot off the accelerator I felt its presence behind me, like a steel tower toppling forward.

"Eventually I turned off to the left, next to the Red Hill Post Office, but the traffic light was green and I can still remember how close the bus seemed as it thundered past, swerving to my side as if it too wanted to make the turn, then changed its mind."

He paused, frowning. "I think it was pale blue that time, but I can't be sure. It has been re-painted several times you know. First blue, I think, then orange, then green. The same colours as all the other buses. That's why I didn't think anything of it that first time."

After the spate the little man seemed uncertain again, hunched and sweating in his ill-fitting grey suit that was far too hot for the Durban summer. He managed to make the comfortable upholstered chair seem like a bar stool, the way he perched nervously on top of it; like a frightened meerkat, ready to duck behind a wall of silence at the first sudden movement or noise.

"Carry on. When did you see it again? I'm sure that's what you came to tell me about." I tried to sound encouraging without being pushy. There's no quicker way to get them to clam up tight than to push too hard and it's not the question that does the damage, it's the tone.

"I remember the second time much more clearly," he said, and he was off at a canter again, the words tumbling out so fast I had difficulty hearing some of them. "It was less than a week later and I had Sally with me. That's my daughter. She's three and I drive much more slowly when she is in the car. It was a weekend, because we were going to the beach. We often go off on our own, just the two of us, but we don't usually go by that route. This time I had to fetch something at a friend's house, her bathing costume I think. It must have been a Sunday because there wasn't much traffic and on a Saturday that road is pretty hectic."

"You saw it on North Coast Road again?"

"Yes. Almost the same spot. This time it was in front of us and I don't think I even noticed anything special about it until we were pretty close. It just seemed bigger, like the first time. I had no idea then that they were the same, of course, but I remember thinking that they were making them wider and wider and it shouldn't be allowed. Higher too. It looked precarious. You know how they lean over on the corners? Well despite being so wide, this one seemed to lean further than the others, as if it was carrying a tremendous load.

"It wasn't going fast either, about fifty or sixty kilometres an hour, which for them is slow. I didn't realise until much later that it wanted me to catch up of course, but I'll come to that just now.

"What happened wouldn't have scared me so much if it hadn't been for the bus behind me, a perfectly ordinary bus, one of those Putco Leylands and it was going like a bat out of hell, like they always do."

The little man's shoulders hunched at the memory and his eyes flashed up and to the left, where the driving mirror would be. "It was while I was looking in the mirror for an instant that it happened. As if it knew my eye was off the road, the bus in front of me stopped. It didn't slow down. It just stopped. No brake lights, no warning. One minute a few tons of steel with half a hundred people on board was travelling at sixty kilometres an hour, the next instant it was stationary."

He was almost going through the motions of driving now, eyes wide at the sight of that wall of steel in front of him, hands fumbling in his lap as if looking for a steering wheel to hold onto – the sweat standing out like blisters among the thinning ginger hairs above his forehead.

"I didn't have time to think. I just swerved." His body moved involuntarily sideways. "To try to stop would have been crazy with that other bus behind me. I went skidding out of control right across the road and by some miracle there was nothing coming the other way. I corrected just short of a parked car, felt my car begin to slide, corrected again and eventually spun around two or three times, finishing on the wrong side of the road and facing the way I had come.

"Sally started to cry. 'Why are you driving so hard, Daddy?' She always said I drove hard when she had to hold on tight when we went around a corner. But she was okay. Nothing broken, nothing bleeding, barely bruised, as far as I could tell.

"By the time I had checked on her and made sure I wasn't a stationary target in the middle of the road, it occurred to me that, unless there was an incredibly talented driver at the wheel of the bus behind me, there should have been an almighty smash as tons of rapidly moving steel collided with the stationary bus in front.

"There hadn't been a crash though, and I could see the back of the ordinary bus disappearing around the corner a few hundred metres away. Of the other bus, the orange one, there was no sign.

"I must admit that I was pretty shaken, but not as shaken then as I am now that I know what is happening. We'd had a rough night the night before and I hadn't got home until the early hours, after putting away a good few over the limit. I think at the back of my mind I believed I might have imagined that bus to be moving one minute and stationary the next. It was certainly frightening enough to make me think I was seeing things.

"What keeps on coming back, however, is that orange wall rushing towards me. It was so close when I swerved that I can remember how the dust had collected thicker near the wheels at the sides than in the middle. You see it wasn't as if it wasn't clear or I can't remember. Every time I saw that bus it became clearer in my mind. Each detail of the vehicle itself is also clear. For example, I can say with confidence that the right-hand back indicator glass was cracked and broken, although how I picked up a detail like that in the split second it took me to swerve I don't know.

"I took Sally home. She performed a bit about not going to the beach, but somehow I couldn't bring myself to carry on down that road in the direction the bus had taken. You can imagine how difficult it was trying to explain to a three-year-old that my car was pointing to what seemed the safest way to go – home.

"I can't remember exactly what I told my wife. I know I said a bus had 'nearly got us', because those are the words she later threw back at me. I suppose it must have been my subconscious speaking, because at that time I was still unaware of any malevolent intent."

He surfaced, as if for air and for a moment I thought the spell which kept him talking might have broken; but then, like a diver determined to get on with an unpleasant job, he plunged back into his story.

"It wasn't until our next encounter that I realised the bus was trying to kill me."

This was the difficult part for him. The crunch. I knew that if he kept talking now he would spill it all. His eyes were flitting everywhere except in my direction and he was sweating seriously now, faced with making admissions that couldn't be considered sane or logical.

"I know I should have said the bus driver was trying to kill me," he blurted out, "but that's not what I feel. I know it is the bus itself that is responsible. It has an identity of its own, a bigness against which my smallness makes me helpless.

"It happened the very next morning. I was on my way to work. I always took that route, you know. Down North Coast Road past the brick factory where the heavy trucks turning sometimes foul things up a bit, but it's still the shortest route for me. There was plenty of traffic as usual just before 7.30, and we were travelling two abreast, although that can be pretty dangerous at times where the road isn't really built to take a bus and a car side by side with traffic coming the other way too.

"This time, the bus came from the other side. I can't say how I knew it was the same bus. It's ridiculous, I know, as this time it was painted that lime green one of the companies uses, but for an incredible moment, before it even showed signs of moving out to overtake the bus next to it, I knew that it was the same one.

"I also knew that it was going to get me. It was going to crush me against the truck I was travelling next to as surely as if I were to be a fly to be smeared against a window pane.

"'It's so wide,' I remember thinking as it came out to overtake. It must have been doing at least ninety kilometres an hour on that slight down-slope. We were travelling slower, almost bumper to bumper and side by side, nowhere to escape past the truckload of bricks on my left.

"I read a book once called Leviathan. It was about a yachtsman who was run down by a supertanker. It described so well his feeling of helplessness when that wall of black steel bore down on him through the whiteness of a storm.

"That's what I felt too, but the wall of steel bearing down on me was a sickly pale green in colour and had the manufacturer's emblem below the windscreen. Just like I remember that broken indicator glass, I should be able to remember the emblem, but I can't. I know it wasn't Leyland, Volvo or Mercedes. It was something I hadn't seen before and yet its shape won't crystallise in my mind.

"I did the only thing I could. I stood on the brakes and pulled into the truck next to me as hard as I could, as if that could lessen the impact on the other side." He leaned the other way in his chair this time, cowering from the memory.

"As the corner of that steel monster hit me I closed my eyes. The impact was incredible. I could feel glass from the windscreen lash my face as my side of the car was subjected to enormous pressure, while at the same time I could hear the left-hand side tearing sickeningly against the truck.

"The worst was on my side, however. I didn't hit the bus head-on, or rather it didn't hit me head-on, as I am sure it was trying to do. Instead it hit me in that smearing motion I was talking about. The one which leaves a translucent red-yellow mess on the window. The green side of the bus simply leaned into me, pushing, smearing and I recall seeing row upon row of black faces flashing past above me, impassive and uncaring.

"Finally there was another impact from behind and I remember thinking that it had all taken so long to happen, yet had been so quick. The shriek of metal, the rain of glass, the mind-numbing forces of deceleration and sudden acceleration again as I was struck from behind, all compressed into a tiny particle of time that still brings me screaming upright in my bed more than five months later.

"I didn't drive for a long time after the accident. I blacked out before I had even stopped moving, I think, but somehow I escaped serious injury. Something had hammered me on the head and I dimly remember loud voices and fingers pointing in accusation as I lay on the bitumen waiting for the ambulance.

"They told me later that the bus didn't stop. Or that's what I thought they were saying. What they were actually saying was that it didn't exist and I don't want ever to believe that. But, you see, I've really got no choice. They let me out of hospital within a week and took me to see my car. The left hand side was scraped raw by that truck, and there was a nasty dent in the back as well. But the right side, where the bus hit it, was completely undamaged.

"Perhaps I should have come to see you then. It would certainly have been the logical thing to do and my wife tried to talk me into it, but I couldn't somehow. You see, I was sure it was just overwork and after a week of sick leave I felt fine again.

"When I did eventually pluck up the courage to start driving again I didn't go along North Coast Road. It wasn't a conscious decision. There is an alternative route and I automatically took it.

"In fact, aside from coming to your office this morning, I haven't driven along North Coast Road since the accident. I think my wife knew, but she didn't say anything. We haven't been talking about things much since she told me she didn't believe in the bus and wanted me to come and see you."

I didn't tell him his wife had already been to see me; had told me of his screaming nightmares; his obsession with avoiding the most logical route to work; his reluctance to drive at all unless it was absolutely necessary; and the gradual breakdown of their relationship when he told her of his paranoia and she could not share his fears.

Now that he had made the admission that he actually believed an inanimate and probably imaginary object – not its driver, mind you, but the bus itself – had it in mind to kill him, he was more relaxed and I knew I wouldn't have to wait for the rest of the story.

"I've only seen the bus once since then and that was last week. This time it was painted dark blue.

"I told you I haven't driven along North Coast Road, didn't I. But you see it isn't as simple as that. Our local café, where we get all our milk and bread, is in North Coast Road.

"I have been able to park around the corner and walk to the café. It felt safe and I thought the bus would never get me unless I was on the road.

"I was wrong. It almost got me again last Friday. I had been at the shops and was coming back with one of those cardboard cartons of milk in one hand and the newspaper in the other, trying to read the headlines as I walked. It was where the pet shop and hardware shop are, a little along from the café. There is a parking area above the pavement in front of the shops and you have to take your chances with people reversing out.

"I think it was the sound that made me look up. It has a deeper sound than other buses. It was coming fast, wheels right up against the pavement, bodywork overhanging by a foot or more. I had no choice but to dive out of the way.

"The milk fell about six inches from my face and the back tyre of a Valiant reversing out exploded the carton like a soggy paper bag, just like it would have exploded my skull, brains like milk squirting on to the tar.

"When I looked up, the bus was pulling off. I caught the white flash of the driver's teeth as he smiled and the anonymous disinterest of the faces in the windows high above me; faces without expression, somehow identical, men and women alike, uniform in their blackness.

"I didn't tell my wife about that incident. I bought another pint of milk elsewhere, well away from North Coast Road and explained my appearance by saying I had tripped and fallen trying to read the paper and walk along the pavement at the same time. It was true in a way.

"I had told her after the accident that I would never see a shrink. Sorry Doc, but that's how I have always thought of psychiatrists. But she gave me your name after the accident and it kept coming to mind, especially after that last incident."

The ordeal of his story over, the little man visibly relaxed.

"I must admit that telling somebody about it has made it all seem a bit silly and I won't blame you if you don't believe a word of what I say." He gave an embarrassed little chuckle. "I'm not sure that I do myself, actually, now that I'm sitting here telling you about it, but it certainly seemed real enough these past five or six months.

"What happens now, Doc?" For a moment he looked worried again. "Now that I've bared my soul, does it mean I'm cured and that it won't come and get me when I walk out that door; or are you going to prescribe drugs and things. I don't mind telling you that I've already tried quite a few you can buy off the shelf."

"I don't think I'm going to prescribe anything," I told him as he rose from his chair, pointedly looking at his watch and making it clear he considered the appointment over – as if he had done his share and now it was up to me.

I was quite frankly puzzled. Mr Graham clearly believed in his bus completely, but aside from the strain associated with this belief, he seemed completely normal. I was going to have to find out a lot more about this patient before I could offer any form of treatment and I told him as much.

After reassurances that the general nature of his problem was more common than he might imagine and it was definitely curable, I suggested a series of appointments beginning the following afternoon.

"Four-thirty will be fine. I can pop off work a bit early and miss the rush hour," he said, offering me a moist and nervous handshake at the door. "But what about the bus,. Doc? Is it for real or am I nuts? I mean, it's one thing to imagine rats in the attic, or bats in the belfry, but a bloody great bus is a bit different. Surely I couldn't have imagined that!"

"Don't worry Mr Graham. For you that bus is as real as the hundreds that thunder past my window every day. What we have to do is discover what makes it so real for you and we'll start on that problem tomorrow," I said in my most reassuring voice.

Mr Graham's appointment had gone over its allotted hour but I hadn't wanted to stop the flow. I buzzed for my next patient and stepped to the window as I waited for the receptionist to usher her in.

One floor down in North Coast Road a black bus was waiting, its deep-throated idle distinct from the background traffic noise. It looked bigger than the other buses somehow, and the emblem in the front window was familiar, although I couldn't make out the detail at that distance.

"It's probably the colour that makes it look so menacing," I thought as I turned to greet my next patient.

CARNIVORE

By Amanda le Bas de Plumetot

She watches from behind glass, a kind of aquarium in reverse. They cruise in like sharks. Sleek metal bodies glide onto the forecourt and pause beside the bowsers, waiting to be fed. Their lights reflect from the wet concrete around them. She stands at her console ignoring the ache in her back, punching a tattoo of instructions into the computer. It shrieks and twitters at her, demanding as much of her attention as the sharks' drivers who come thrusting money or credit cards at her.

In the ocean of paused traffic he moves with swift intelligence, sitting head and shoulders above the blank, cold panels of metal and glass that surround him. He sees the cars' inhabitants staring with dead fish eyes at the red light that frustrates their progress and he laughs as he passes them. His thighs are pistons driving the pedals that move his wheels. The reflective plastic of his helmet is visible as he checks the intersection and then goes through, riding the wave of right-turning traffic.

She counts the day's take, preparing to close her shift, grabbing at seconds as her impatient customers throw money at her, or tie their names in knots at the bottom of printed statements. She smiles as the next shift comes to take over. Frustration in the queue mounts a little as the computer pauses to print out shift totals but she doesn't care. Soon she'll be joining them, merging with the throng. Going home.

He slides between their dangerous hulks and veers the wrong way down a one-way one street, safe for a little while. Nothing follows him but the hiss of his wheels on the wet road. He sometimes detects looks of pity when the weather's bad, but he loves riding in the rain. He can feel steam rising off his thighs. He licks the rain that runs down his face. He's made it slightly salty.

She emerges from the fishbowl of the petrol station shop and climbs into the cold damp interior of her car. She twists the key and feels metal pulse into life around her. Lights reflect off the road and in a moment she joins the gliding shoal all headed for home. As she stops for a red light, the car's warmth begins to creep around her ankles and finally her feet begin to ache. For the past eight hours she's been standing behind that console. Lunch was a packet of out-of-date chips with salty change for the customers. She's reassured by aching feet; it means they're no longer numb. In her mind there is a picture of her children waiting for her, the TV's turned on, the homework's open and ignored on the table, dirty dishes clutter the kitchen. She'll stop for pizza on the way home and they'll all be happy.

The trees are getting lost now in the darkening sky. He doesn't mind. All seasons are good. He loves being part of the landscape, not just driving through it. The smell of fresh-fallen autumn leaves makes him think of new earth. He can hear the blare of TVs and kids' voices as he passes by their houses. It reminds him that he's going home too. Every bit of his trip has a different smell, a different sound. He emerges out of Burnt Cabbage Street and glides into Fried Onion Avenue. Soft rain patters his face and beats a tattoo on his helmet.

She stretches in her seat. Years ago, she learned to stop hating her job. The money comes in as regular as the petrol price rise before the weekend. It makes a difference to her. The school holidays are coming and she is planning a trip. It's only down to the bay, but she showed the kids the caravan park brochure and they're already excited. She's been working extra shifts and saving so that they can eat fish and chips and go to the movies and buy toys. They won't be kids forever. She wants to make the most of these ephemeral years.

He's cut a whole chunk out of his trip home, through the back streets. Now he returns to the highway. Back into the traffic. He passes a bus and it passes wind, farting a black, dinosaur emission at him. He emits a little methane of his own and thrusts his orange, reflective, organically-powered machine down the lane of creeping predators. At this time of night he's particularly wary, it's been a long day. Like fractious beasts they're inclined to charge and he'd sooner not be in their way.

It gets dark so early this time of year. She imagines the kids at home with the dark creeping up on them. She has to turn right through a slow intersection. Cars in front of her pause as if waiting for the green light to be well and truly warm before they accept it and move on. Her foot stabs the accelerator and jabs the brake. She could have been through on that change if those idiots hadn't been so slow.

The muscles in his legs are beginning to cramp. The cold's seeping in. The hill up to the intersection isn't steep, but it's long. He sees the lights changing to red but he surges through, taking advantage of the ponderous inertia the cars always show at green lights.

She sees the cross-lights turning to red. She knows this intersection, it will be her green arrow next and she leaps into her turn, aware only a moment later that there's something already in her space. Her foot hits the brake and her ankle flexes and bends the wrong way. The tyres skid in the wet and her foot slips completely off the brake pedal.

She hears the thud and the smash and there's a sudden crazing of her windscreen. There are screaming, awful sounds and she isn't sure who's making them. She hears horns and screeching brakes and at once she's surrounded with light cast by the accusing eyes of dozens of cars, all staring at her. She opens the door and has to lean on it because her right ankle doesn't work any more.

The bike lies like bare bones, bitten and crushed beneath the wheels. His reflective silver shimmers in the light, settling like a drift of scales onto the water. He lies, torn and broken, smashed into the chrome teeth of her car. He paints the sea about him red; his pumping, thrusting body emits a final spurt of hot, wet energy into the carnivore's mouth.

ARE WE THERE YET?

By Marica Salpietro

No, we are not there yet.

You only asked me two minutes ago.

Yes, Andy, it was only two minutes ago.

I know what will make the time go fast. Why don't we play "I Spy"?

What do you spy, Andy?

Something beginning with "h"?

Let's see – "house"?

What about "horses"?

What about "humans"?

Yes, all right, I give up.

A hippopotamus? Where did you see a hippopotamus, Andrew?

But you're not supposed to imagine it.

Because the game is called "I Spy", not "I Imagine".

Who told you that rules are meant to be broken?

Is this the same Jeffery who told you he had an elephant in his back yard?

Andy, did you ever see Jeffery's elephant?

No, I'm not calling Jeffery a liar. I'm not calling Jeffery anything. I think it's my turn to spy something. Let's see. I Spy with my little eye something beginning with "c".

No, you can't imagine things beginning with "c".

"Sky" doesn't start with the letter c".

Do you really think mummy can spy a camel?

Yes, it would be fun to ride a camel.

No, we can't ride a camel today.

Because we are going to grandma's today.

I know you'd prefer to ride a camel, but don't you want to see grandma?

Well, I'm sure she'd like to see you.

No, Andy, we can't pretend grandma's a camel.

Because that's not nice.

Stop sulking, Andy.

Yes, you can open the window.

Open it just a little.

I said a little.

Andrew! Stick your head back inside the car!

No, you cannot do it again.

Andrew, close the window. You don't want your sister to catch a cold, do you?

Well, I don't want her to catch a cold.

No, we can't put Mallory in the boot.

Because it's dark in there.

Do you think she can use a torch by herself?

We don't call people by those names, Andrew. She's only a baby, that's why she can't operate a torch.

No, she can't use matches either.

I don't think a gas lamp would fit in the boot.

No, we can't pull over and try.

Because we'll be late for grandma's.

Andrew, I thought I told you to go before we left.

Yes I did.

Did you clean your ears this morning?

No, don't clean them now. It's just an expression.

Mallory's jacket isn't for cleaning your ears, Andrew.

I know you still need to go, but you'll have to wait until we get to grandma's house.

I don't have any water.

No, we cannot stop to get some.

No, I don't think you'll die of thirst.

Andy, that's Mallory's milk bottle, not yours.

I know you need to use the toilet but you'll have to wait.

Well, try not to think about it.

I know, lets play "I Spy" again. I spy with my little eye something beginning with "t".

No, it's not a toilet.

No, it's not a tap either.

What are those things growing by the side of the road with leaves?

Where do you see a turtle?

Just a little further, Andy.

Ten minutes.

Yes, then you can use the toilet.

And have a drink.

Just down that road there. Do you see the road with the traffic lights?

Mallory is not blocking your view.

No, you can't come up to the front.

You can see a lot of things from the back.

But Mallory likes it in the back, why don't you like it?

Stop calling your sister names.

No, sit still.

I told you already, you can't come up to the front.

No, we can't exchange places.

Because I have to drive.

Maybe when you turn eighteen.

No you can't have a practice shot.

Andy, stop that and fasten your seat belt.

Sit down.

Stop hitting Mallory.

No, she did not start it.

How could Mallory have jumped out of her seat and hit you?

But I was watching.

Oh, Andy, I do hope you will behave for grandma this afternoon.

No, Andy, we are not going to the zoo.

I know you prefer monkeys to grandma, but the monkeys don't give you nice hugs and warm chocolate milk cookies.

Yes, you are right, grandma doesn't swing from trees.

We are nearly there. Have you got your shoes and socks on?

But grandma likes you looking like a little gentleman.

I know you are not a little gentleman, but we are going to pretend.

No, it isn't the same thing as lying.

What do you mean you only have one sock?

Look under the seat.

I didn't say look under Mallory. Stop making trouble Andy.

Why would Mallory have it in her nappy?

Ah, I told you it was under the seat didn't I?

No, we don't have time to play sock puppets.

Andrew, please put the sock on.

All right, please put Mr Sam Smelly Sock on your foot.

Now, let's check everything before we get out.

Socks and shoes?

Excellent.

Shoelaces tied?

Very Good.

No, leave your crayons in the car.

Leave Elmo too, please.

No, Elmo won't be bored. I'm sure Elmo will amuse himself.

Right, let's go.

Don't you want to use the toilet?

Oh I see, you don't need to go anymore.

Yes, you will still need to get out of the car.

Wait by the curb while I unbuckle your sister.

That doesn't mean ring the doorbell!

Andrew!

It just takes her a little longer to come to the door.

I don't know, let's ring it again.

Yes, grandma may not be wearing her hearing aid.

I don't know where she is.

All right, let's ring it once more.

No, we can't go to the zoo to look for her.

Come on, Andy.

Yes, back in the car please.

We are going home.

Now you need to use the toilet again?

Well, you'll have to wait until we get home.

I didn't have any water before, did I?

Let's have some quiet time, Andy.

I know you don't like quiet time, but let's see how long we can make it last.

No, Mummy has had enough of "I Spy."

Leave your sister alone!

Sit still. Look out the window.

Yes, Andy?

No, we are not there yet.

PAIN

By J. A. Kent

He drove constantly, day and night – seldom resting, the truck the only world that he knew or cared for.

Night –

Headlights flooding the bitumen ahead, pouring into the darkness and spilling over the edge of the road, chasing shadows into the night. The dash-dash of centre road white lines racing towards him hypnotically, sliding from sight beneath the truck. Nocturnal wanderers, rabbits or kangaroos mostly, either fatally mesmerised by the probing headlights or else scrambling desperately for the shadows. Suicidal insects splattering the windscreens, brief punctuation marks erased by the pumping windscreen wipers.

He rarely slept; there were too many ghosts.

He drove, they said of him, as though there was no tomorrow!

He drove, he knew, because there were tomorrows that the faceless ghosts wouldn't allow him to forget...

The north run – from south to the sunshine state; an overload of canned beer for a Queensland brewery, the return-trip produce for the southern market, bananas and mangos. A five-day round trip for most drivers, he was back and unloaded in three.

It was raining –

Silvery streaks lashing out of the darkness, colliding with the windscreen and exploding like miniature water bombs before being punched to oblivion by the sweeping wipers. Water glistening on the bitumen, reflecting the headlights into twisting arcs of light skywards, peripheral rainbows of light dancing in the rain.

The girl was standing by the roadside, beneath a streetlight, her thumb raised. He would not have stopped only he had slowed to drive through Maisden; he always did. Still, he wondered why he did stop. He never picked up hitchhikers.

Clambering into his cocoon of light. Jeans and T-shirt and a pullover tied around her waist. A small overnight bag. Hair bedraggled, a bead of water hanging from the point of her nose, her face stained. Rainwater or tears?

"Going far?"

"Queensland."

About seventeen, he guessed, the same age Meredith would have been –

Seven years ago.

Meredith, on school holidays and excited about the promised truckie trip with her father. Her mother not wanting her to go, she was too young, but he insisting. The Shingleback – wet that night too – a winding road from the top of the mountain down into Leigh Valley. Good bitumen, wide, with safety ramps, no threat at all to an experienced truckie, and he was the best. The blinding high-beam lights and a car slewing towards him…

His hands crushed the steering wheel.

Remembering now –

He couldn't avoid the impending collision. The edge of the road was too close and he lost control of the rig. He remembered his anger. The frustration and the fear came afterwards.

The edge of the mountain road, weakened by rain, crumbling beneath the weight of the rig; the truck rolling; the distant sound of his daughter's awakening scream.

Her scream would remain with him forever.

He was injured, his daughter killed. Unhurt, the other driver was exonerated. An accident, they said, a combination of wet roads and bad luck. Only he knew that it was the other driver's fault, but they wouldn't listen to him. An accident, they repeated, yet still the finger of guilt pointed at the truckie, it always did.

A fortnight after the coroner's decision his wife had suicided. She couldn't live with the killer of their only child! "Killer!" her accusation burned painfully deep.

They were with him now, as always, the ghosts, in the cabin, leering at him, silently taunting him...

"Are you from Maisden, lass?" he asked.

A slight hesitation, then a faint affirmative.

"A bad night for hitching." Tongue in cheek. "You're not running away from home, are you?"

"Y – yes." Her answer surprised him.

"Why?"

"My father, he's a ... monster!'

A hunch she wanted to talk.

"Because he said no to something you wanted to do?"

"I wanted to go to a disco, but it's not the first time. He still treats me like a little girl."

"You're his only daughter?"

"Yes."

"Then perhaps you are still his little girl?"

The girl hesitated.

"Do you have a daughter, mister?"

"I did, she would have been about your age. If she had wanted to go discoing at seventeen I probably would have said no."

"Then you would be a monster too."

Monster? Did this child have any idea what a monster really was?

"No," he said quietly, "not a monster. I would have said no because I cared and wanted to keep her safe, because she was very special to me, still my little girl. I believe that my daughter would have asked me why, though. Did you ask your father why?"

"No." Almost a whisper. "What happened ... your daughter?"

"She died." His voice broke. "An accident."

"You killed her!" His wife screaming at him. Distraught, stricken with pain and hurting that he could do nothing to help her. "You murdered my baby girl!"

"On the Shingleback."

The wheels seemed to hum, or was it the ghosts?

"I'm sorry." For a while she remained silent. Asleep, he decided. She blew her nose. Crying?

"What's your name, girl?" At the top of the Shingleback now.

A slight hesitation, then almost a whisper: "Meredith."

Suddenly shivering, cold, his hands clammy. The ghosts there again, leering at him, silent, knowing smiles that mocked.

Meredith, the same name as his daughter, the same age. He had picked her up in Maisden. Coincidence, nothing more. Still, the question had to be asked.

"Your surname ... is it ...Wentworth?"

A long pause. Finally, faintly, "Yes."

Dear God!

Downhill, the gear box in forgotten low gear screaming in protest, the wipers beating frantically against the rain-spattered windscreen, the cabin suddenly too hot. Perspiration, trickling down his back, his face wet. A pain in his chest, a tightening band of steel crushing his lungs, his breathing sharp, ragged. Hands fiercely gripping the steering, the accelerator pedal hot against the sole of his boot.

A roadside sign: Trucks use low gear.

Hayden Wentworth of Maisden!

The man who had driven that other vehicle, responsible for the death of his daughter, indirectly for that of his wife. The driver who had sentenced him to the agony of a personal hell filled with recriminations reaching at him from beyond the grave, the faceless taunting ghosts and the pain that never ever went away.

Wentworth attempting to apologise. He knew how the truckie would feel. He had a daughter himself the same age – coincidentally the same name – Meredith.

How could he know?

But now, Meredith Wentworth, beside him, riding a truck down Shingleback, on a dark and wet night, as it had been seven years ago!

Meredith Wentworth, a hunched silhouette in the light reflecting from the dash. And others too, in the cabin – the ghosts, their silent laughter heard only by him ringing in his ears. Urging now, as they had for seven long years, towards the high-speed plunge over the edge of the mountain, to the anguish and suddenness and explosiveness of violent death.

He has always resisted them. Death was too final, he believed, there was no reunion with past loved ones. Ashes to ashes...

Manipulating the gear stick, cogs shifting upwards. The speedo needle flickering higher – the truck swaying –– tyres screeching – clawing bitumen on the steep downward curves.

Perhaps now?

She was his passenger – Meredith Wentworth, on the Shingleback where his daughter had died because of the carelessness of her father. Ahead the Devil's Elbow, that worst part of the Shingleback where the road almost turned back to look at itself and where the drop on the off-driver's side was almost a hundred metres sheer. A tree, that night, had stopped the truck from going over, a tree would not stop him tonight.

The truck swaying, tyres still loudly protesting, a high load striking the roadside overhang. The unseen forces urging: destroy this young woman, this child the same age as Meredith would have been. Take her with you over Devil's Elbow – to an end to personal pain but the beginning of another's. Hayden Meredith to know the anguish and the suffering and the pain of having his only daughter wrenched so violently and so permanently from him.

The speedo needle staggered higher. The girl did not notice the speed or the swaying of the truck.

They remained, the ghosts, between him and the girl, crowding his cabin with their taunts, goading him on to certain death, accusing fingers jabbing at him.

He smiled.

But then, suddenly, a face...

A small round face with sad staring eyes. Meredith, his Meredith, shaking her head the way that she would when he did or said something "silly". She wasn't screaming now but her face was wet – tears. Was Meredith crying, for him?

"Meredith!"

Releasing the steering wheel and reaching for her. Nothing! The ghosts were gone to – now only a space of darkness between himself and his passenger, an endless void. Outside, the buffeting wind seemed to pause for breath.

A new frightening thought – a reality driven home with a violence that left him exhausted.

He couldn't take this girl with him, he couldn't destroy another child!

Even if it meant an end to his personal hell!

Too late to reverse the decision? The headlights flashed across the U-shaped Line and Arrow on a road sign. The Devil's Elbow was only a corner away!

A maelstrom of madness, unreality that closed and smothered and threatened, then tearing apart in a violence of gear box and brakes and engine resisting yet responding. Praying for a miracle though he believed in no God – and the miracle happening. The mechanical monster lurching as if by instinct into the safety ramp, surging upwards slowing – gears crashing, brakes screaming – stopping.

Silence, then –

"Brake trouble," he told her when she asked why they had stopped.

They reached the bottom of the Shingleback in early daylight yet the perspiration still soaking his shirt. The girl asked to be let off in the town. She was going home, she said, she had been stupid.

"Don't hitchhike," he told her, giving her fifty dollars for breakfast and train fare.

"You can pay me back when next I pass through Maisden."

A hesitation, sad-cow eyes regarding him solemnly.

"My name isn't Meredith … and I'm not Wentworth."

She had taken the Christian name from that painted on the bonnet of his truck, Wentworth, because he had suggested it. Nor was she from Maisden but from Toomey, a little further down the highway. She had hitched to Maisden.

Dear God! He was gaping at her.

Did the name Wentworth mean something? She queried. No, he said.

She smiled and walked away, towards the post office, to the bank of telephone boxes outside the building.

Why was it suddenly so cold?

The mist of rain was lifting away from the Shingleback to a glow in the east. Sunrise, a new day, yet somehow it still seemed grey, foreboding…

Suddenly THEY were there again!

The ghosts, the spectres, the shadows, whatever they were. Faceless blobs briefly, then leering devil-like faces crowding into the cabin with him, crushing him with their taunts, their accusations, the pointing fingers. It was as if they had played some immense joke on him, tested his resolve and exposing his weakness, suggesting cruelly that he had somehow failed.

"Go away!"

He couldn't breathe.

"Coward!" they taunted. He feared the suddenness and completeness of a death that would forever end the pain.

"Coward!"

He revved the truck, violently, blindly finding gears, feeling it move, jerk, hearing the high side scraping a lamppost.

"Damn you!" he screamed.

The girl heard the truck and looked out of the telephone box, waving to the driver in his high cabin.

Strange, she thought, why had he turned around? Why was he driving back the way that he had come, towards the Shingleback?

Had he forgotten something?

WHILE HE'S DRIVING

By Liliane Grace

I thought this was supposed to be a holiday. She looked across at his granite profile and then sighed back to her passenger window. Shrubby trees, red dirt and vast yellow-green plains blurred steadily past. He had not said a word for two towns. And New South Wales was longer than she had ever imagined.

She slept, her legs crookedly tucked against the door, her head rammed into the corner between the armrest and his seat. They bumped and jolted across New South Wales. Waking with a stiff neck, she wondered if he had even glanced at her, but no … his eyes were still tied unblinkingly to some ever-distant point on the horizon.

Gathering her legs, elbows, blanket, bag and stray tissues, she struggled into a sitting position. Her gaze landed on the ruthless grey road and shrubby trees red dirt vast yellow-green plains. She looked sideways: the same nose and mouth, the prickly chin and hands set firmly on the wheel. Her sigh was cut in two by a bump.

Later Something Happened. The clouds acquired a leaden shade and the weather became drippy grey. He slowed down for a town and for a few minutes her eyes raked the motels, the pub, the park, the service stations and shops as they passed through the empty streets. Wet town gone from view, they rattled across a primitive bridge and bingo: shrubby trees red dirt vast yellow-green plains. It began to pour; a monotonous black arm cut across her vision smearing drips one ways and wiping them off the other. New South Wales was all grey.

The puncture was inevitable. She stood uselessly on the side of the road, arms folded across her chest, watching uninterestedly the intermittent line of cars that appeared on the crest of the hill and then hurtled past them. At her feet, metal clanking sounds and grunts accompanied the tyre-changing process. At least it had stopped raining – It's done? She climbed back in, settling on lumpily folded blanket and thrusting the junk at her feet forwards. The engine stuttered, yawned, and they were off. It was warmer in here. She sighed and surrendered to yet another stretching silence.

For a while they coincided with a rusty-looking railway line. She imagined the trip by train. There was a yard full of bright red and yellow factory machines. Some tin sheds. A huge crashing ("F**k! Didn't see that") pot hole, and another town unrolled its beautiful wares. Little old-style houses, a self-important church building, and some real country people walking across the road to the pub. He pulled into a service station to fill up and take away toasted cheese sandwiches and coffee. Back into her familiarly uncomfortable seat and they rode out of town.

As the rain started again.

They were stuck for two hills behind an old canvas-wrapped truck that groaned its way up, wheezing black smoke, which passed straight through their vents into the car. She put her hand over her nose and he chose that moment to turn and look at her. He smiled (at her) and turned back to the road. She dropped her hand exhaustedly. The truck had thrust itself over the crest and was now flinging downhill. They passed it.

There was a For Sale sign offering someone an anonymous expanse of shrubby trees, red dirt and vast yellow-green plains. She closed her eyes for a moment and opened them at the next town. "We're halfway," he said, and she gasped inwardly. All of that again?

The other half of New South Wales was grey too.

She took a swig out of her bottle of water and spilt some down her chest. He chose that moment to turn and look at her.

Their eyes met and parted. She dabbed. He wiped his forehead with the back of his hand, grimaced, stretched his neck, sighed, and settled back into the granite mould.

They had been travelling for hours and hours and hours.

All of her internal organs had been quivering for hours and hours and hours. Every now and then they hit such a bump that she had to catch her breasts on their way down.

She looked at those poor old cows standing on clumpy grass in the drizzling wet. A bit further on there were some dirty little sheep. A brown symmetrical dam. A homestead. An arrow that way: caravan park.

Old Granite Face continued to follow the broken white line.

The heavy clouds were gathering, preparing to tuck the earth in for the night. It was a nurturing feeling.

More trucks than she'd ever seen in her life. They'd spent last night on the side of the road with trucks. Waking up, she was cramped and dying for a piss, and her hair was tangled. The morning was streaky yellow and beautiful. One by one the trucks had eased out. He woke up, lifting his head off her arm and running his fingers through his hair. A stretch, a series of yawns, a puddle in the dirt by the tyre and they were off. Well, it had been an experience.

He clicked on the radio and when the crackle died down they had the pleasure of hearing one song followed by six commercials and the news reliably each half hour. The usual spate of government promises and denials, criminal activities and trivia. So this is civilization, she thought.

She looked to her left: the earth was eclipsing their view of the sun, providing the time-honoured illusion that it "set", sinking "beneath the edge" of a flat earth. Lead-bottomed clouds trailed pink and yellow scarves against the dusky sky. As she watched, the colours merged and thinned to a line across the horizon that burned orange. The last light extinguished and man-made substitutes blinked to life, poking holes in the darkness. They drove resolutely on.

She forced her body into yet another unnatural reclining position and closed her eyes. He must have unwound a window because a cold and noisy wind blew in suddenly, circling around her ears and neck and down her back. She clawed around for her blanket and the car rocked its way through the night, the wind rushing loudly past. Opened her eyes at one point and was startled by an enormous number of stars glittering against the black sky. The Milky Way was the only thing she recognised.

It was funny to think that people or things probably lived on those stars. Light years ago, of course.

"Queensland," he said, and she jerked herself excitedly into a sitting position. They clattered across the bridge into the streets of the border town.

Climbed out of the car and it was warm, actually warm. A bus was pouring a river of people into the service station's cafe. By the time the bus travellers had finished all that was left were pies and sticky bars. He was dripping weariness as they walked around looking for food; she was bouncing.

They tackled their sleeping quarters. She glanced curiously into the noisy, bursting pub lounge as they finally made their way upstairs with their bags in hand. They had been allocated the "unit", which even possessed its own bathroom. He unlocked the door and she looked in. A balcony room jutting over the street with large, curtained windows and two single beds.

She wasn't tired (she had dozed for most of the way) she wanted to talk and savour her first experience of Queensland. There were people walking around in the streets, visible when they passed beneath a light, and definitely it felt warmer and more holiday-ish than anywhere else so far. Behind her the toilet flushed. She gazed around enthusiastically before letting the curtain drop and turning back to the room. He was undressing, and then he kissed her, hugged her, and climbed into one of the beds. After a moment he sighed and the bed creaked as he shifted his weight and then she knew he was already asleep.

Well...

She looked around at the enamel basin and old-fashioned dresser, at the mirror and back to where he lay warmly enfolded into himself. She could hear his regularly spaced breaths in and out and the bed's occasional creaks. She wondered about going downstairs and decided against it.

Staring outside. The warm air ... and an excitement pervaded this place. There was a whole state between herself and her home.

Voices burst onto the balcony and for a breathless moment she wondered if they would walk in. He had lifted his head, instantly awake and on guard, and then, when nothing happened, dropped it again and returned to sleep. There was music playing now, and the voices continued. A couple of youths crashed down the stairs of the hotel entrance and stood beneath her window talking.

"Aren't you going to switch the light off?" he grunted into his pillow.

She withdrew from the window and moved over to the door. Someone on the balcony laughed suddenly; they sounded very near. Neon light from street lamps and signs replaced the contribution of the single globe. As she undressed she wondered what would happen if one of the men on the balcony came into the room.

Climbing into bed, she began imagining, instead, that he (her husband) had abducted her and they were travelling across the country and she couldn't escape because ... because she was ... it was in those days when women had no will of their own. And now he lay sleeping in the other bed, too exhausted to even make any demand of her, and she sat on the edge of her bed clutching the sheets in one hand and gazing and wondering...

She slid between the sheets and her fantasy melted into a dream.

At some early hour she awoke to hear raucous voices and shouting outside. Her body felt warm; she curved and arched sensuously, imagining things…

"Are you awake?" he asked and suddenly she was. Wide awake. It was bright and airy and Queensland stood in this room and everywhere outside.

He went to the toilet, and as he passed her bed on his way back she caught his hand and seduced him into joining her.

His body's message was clearly "We haven't got time…", but he gradually mingled with hers his fingers and thighs and tongue until, clutching her shoulders with eyebright staring, he heaved in as close as he could and then lay on her, enfolding her and caressing her.

They separated kissingly, softly, and turned themselves over to the iron bed that would again carry them along a narrow jolting road between (probably) shrubby trees, red dirt, vast yellow-green plains.

She settled her limbs into the obvious ruts and folded her hands expectantly. The engine raged briefly and settled also, into its even kilometre-munching pace. They exchanged smiles, steadily moving out of town into a surprisingly blue-skied day, and when she next looked at him, his face had slipped into its old granitous curves.

I don't think I'll go on a "driving holiday" with you again, she thought, turning away lumpily to stare outside.

She had been captured … and now he was taking her far away to some … to …

"Cactus," he said, pointing.

… Some cabin in the tropics where…

She gave up. Anyway, there were interesting stilt houses along here. And even palm trees. And the sky was so, so blue.

A four-wheel-drive overtook them: dead black animals were hanging by their feet from a bar and they had been split open revealing…

"What are they?"

"Wild pig."

Ugh! She watched the things swing out of sight. A delicious mental shiver passed over her … it made this seem like a dangerous place, a place where anything might happen…

"Would you mind winding your window up? I'm getting a chill down my neck."

She wound up the window. She sat and stared outside. They drove and drove. She stirred restlessly. He drove. She stared at green trees and blue sky. He drove. She went into trance staring. He was in trance driving. There were many, many kilometres. She rolled her blanket up and thumped it against the door and leaned on it. He drove. They stopped for petrol. He drove. She gazed. She ate. She put tapes on and clicked them over. She dreamed. He drove. She.

"Brisbane," he said, five years later.

She sat up and peered.

"Sleep with someone friendly tonight," a Homestead sign proclaimed.

"I'd rather stay at Flag," the next one interjected.

"Where?" she asked.

"We're in the suburbs."

"Oh." She looked about intelligently.

Soon after, they parked outside their nice little motel room and carried their bags inside. He lay on the neat tan-striped bed with a huge sigh and then didn't move.

She observed her deflated husband for a small moment, biting her fingernails, then climbed onto the bed and lay down beside him. She watched the ceiling do nothing for a while.

He was rolling over and cuddling into her side, fast asleep. He was doing his contented sigh.

"Robert," she said sweetly.

"Mmmmm…"

"See you later, Robert."

"Mmmmm…"

He appeared in the doorway as she was starting the car. "Where are you going?"

"To look around."

"Well, wait a minute. I'll come with you."

He disappeared, scratching his tousled hair. She sat tapping the steering wheel, engine running, her lipstick fresh. He walked to the driver's door automatically. She gazed up at him expectantly, firmly ensconced. "I'll drive."

"Oh. All right." He walked the unfamiliar distance around the bonnet to the passenger seat and heaved into it.

"Where are we going?" "You tell me. I haven't been here before, remember." She eased down the drive.

"Oh…" he scratched his head. "I suppose we should drive into town."

I suppose we should drive into town. Perhaps she would abduct him, she thought, joining the stream of traffic. He was sitting with his hands in his lap and gazing outside. He looked slightly uncomfortable.

She could drive off to some exotic tropical hideaway and … and then stop driving, and thrust the keys into the earth and drag him inside and make love PASSIONATELY while rain dripped from thick green leaves outside the window and…

She looked across at him. He was sleeping.

JUST US

By Vicki Thornton

He drives. He always does. He drives carefully, both hands gripping the steering wheel, thick fingers spread. Gold signet ring embedded in the flesh. Solitude travels with them. The car silent but for the purr of the air-conditioner and his heavy breathing, each breath rasping over buried emotions. And the humming. He hums under his breath. Not loud enough to cause comment but low enough so that it irritates.

Her face is turned to the window and she watches the world pass her by.

It's summer. Heat dances in waves, beats against the rocky outcrops. Shimmers seductively, offers the hope of peace, yet never delivers. The road they travel is narrow, winds its way through dry grass as bleached as the rocks. A landscape of greys and browns, where silence hangs heavy. Every word sampled and tasted before spoken. You can smell the heat, the dry dustiness that invades every pore. Soaks in to become as one, and just as dry and bleached.

And with them comes the river. It hugs the road tenderly, sometimes no more than a dark green trace amongst the rocks. Other times it glistens playfully, tempting with its wetness. Sleek and diamond rare.

The sky is a pale blue, as scoured as the ground beneath it and just as empty. The heat has bleached it of cloud and bird. It stretches from hill to hill. Drawn tight, without any ease, without any breath. In her eyes it becomes the colour of pain.

They drive on. She wants a drink, looks longingly at the river below them. Wishes to stop, to rest her tired head under the cooling shadow of a tree. To escape the icy crispness inside this metal box. She wants to shut her eyes against the dust and emptiness, she has seen too much already.

He points to the distance, there he says, there they found gold. He slaps her thigh, his meaty hand rests briefly, fingers tighten then release. His hand returns to the wheel, and not once has the humming stopped.

They spend the nights at small country towns. Towns with no claim to fame, with stark emptiness that echoes the dwellers' eyes. I'm showing her the country, he says. His voice too loud, his manner too familiar. One hand lands on her shoulder, squeezes just a bit too hard. Married twenty years and she's never been out of the state, he says. Shakes his head at the injustice. Wanted to go overseas, he laughs – overseas, he repeats, the hand squeezes harder. Her eyes seek the safety of her drink. Watches the ice clink in her lemon squash as he orders another beer.

His voice dominates the room and she hunches over in embarrassment. Married for twenty years, he says, you get less for murder. His florid face shines greasily under the fluorescent lights. Just us, he says, smiles wetly with his lips. No children, women's problems, you know. Nods sagely as the other customers refuse to meet his eyes. But she's got me, he says, holds his hands wide, shrugs in boyish imitation.

Her head dips lower, colour flushes her cheeks. Not of embarrassment but of anger. She thinks to before, of clinical rooms, of foreign apparatus, of tests and probing pains. Then of nothing. No child had ever grown inside her barren womb.

They eat in the small dining room. Faded red chairs and walls covered in flyspecked prints of a dry and dusty land. He eats quickly, steak oozing blood. She nibbles, picks at scorched chicken and limp salad.

Outside their room, the night dark and distant, the generator comes to life. It roars with a passion that inspires. His hand rubs her thigh. She wants a hug, a kiss, a rekindling of why they had married. He wants a woman and she's there.

In their bed, she lies back, thinks of the boy she had married. He pounds into her, soft flesh hitting the mattress. He comes quickly, he always does. She rolls over, wraps her arms around her body, trying to ease the emptiness inside.

They drive on the next day. Drive as stubbled hills with cattle give way to bleached sheep that fight the land amongst the rocks. That's the Tambo River he says. She nods, knowing he can't see, her face turned to the window, seeing nothing but a dryness that speaks so eloquently.

KNIGHT OF THE ROAD

By Judy Buckingham

Last spring, when I was fourteen, it all got a bit heavy.

There was this guy I was sort of keen on and he started making up to this two-faced bitch I thought was my best friend. Also, one of the teachers was picking on me, about homework and talking in class and that. Usually, if I tell Mum about something wrong at school, she's off like a hurricane straight into them: teachers, the Head, anyone till they're all running scared of her. This time, all she said was she had enough trouble with Centrelink trying to mess with her pension, thank you, get out of her hair, and I probably deserved it anyway.

I suppose I didn't handle it too well and I thought I might nick off for the day. I packed my denim skirt into my schoolbag, got the bus into the City, changed my clothes in the ladies' and pretended I was sixteen and free to do what I pleased. I only planned to be gone until the end of school time, but after I'd mooched about the shops for a spell I got bored, and I got it into my head that it might be cool to hitch a ride up north. Make them all feel sorry when they missed me.

It was easy to begin with. I made a couple of long rides right off and come tea time I was well upstate in one of those deadhole towns that have a median strip, a town clock and stuff all else, except pubs.

I had just enough money on me for some chips and a Coke at a milk bar, and I parked myself on the steps of some big building – I don't know, town hall, library – anyway, something official. It was getting cold. I only had my denim jacket over a T-shirt. Also it was awful quiet. There were about three men and a dog alive in the place. The only cars around just seemed to be stopping at the pub or the shops. I'd counted on finding an overnight hauler and sleeping in the cabin on the way, but here nothing moved except this bloody motorbike phut-phutting round and round with a couple of guys on the back. They whistled when they came past, but that was all. Never mind. It wasn't that late. The sun was still up and I acted like I didn't give a stuff what time it was, and scrunched up my chip bucket sort of slow and casual.

Then this guy came out the building I was sitting outside of and walked up to me. I thought, he's going to tell me not to chuck litter, keep Australia beautiful and all that crap. And I was going to tell him to mind his own, but all he said was: "You right, mate? You look perished sitting there."

"Sure, I'm fine."

"Where you headed?"

"What's it to you?"

"Not a thing, except I'm going down to Melbourne if you need a ride. I've some business to see to first, but I'll be finished up in about twenty minutes, half an hour if you want to wait."

"Going to Sydney. But thanks."

"Suit yourself," he said and disappeared into a hotel. Business my foot. Wouldn't have gone with him anyway. All the same I didn't fancy hanging around any longer, so I started to leg it out of town.

The road was just dead. Two cars went by and neither pulled over. I'd gone past the last house that I could see just as the sun went down, and I was thinking that maybe I might go back and see if that guy was still around when this old junk heap rattled alongside me. There were two blokes inside, sweaty types in black T-shirts, and the one who wasn't driving had tattoos all over the arm he had hanging out the window. They slowed right down and kept driving level with me. I could count the pimples on Tattoo-arm's neck even in that dim light.

They went on hassling me for five minutes or so, calling out and whistling and that, and then Tattoo-arm said, "Hey you, hop in."

I told him to piss off, and walked on, not looking at them.

Another car went by, but it didn't stop either and I was beginning to feel scared because these two were bumping up and down real close, cocking fingers in the air and swearing, and it was pretty well dark by now. They came nearer and suddenly Tattoo-arm reaches right out and grabs my arm and pulls me up to the car which is still going, so I have to run or get my arm yanked off. I'm swearing and yelling by this, and he's laughing fit to bust and digging his nails in my arm until it really hurts. I can smell grog on his breath so's it nearly turns my stomach. When they braked and let me go, I fell down, and when they got out I nearly wet myself. I screamed and I kicked and I bit Tattoo-arm, and then he hit me on the face, and the other twisted my arm up my back, and I just thought I'd really had it, this was the end of the world, when everything stopped,and I went flop, onto the gravel.

It was shock, I suppose, but it was all a blur for a while. I didn't know what was happening. I sort of realised there was another car because I saw the lights, and there was a lot of shouting, but I couldn't think straight until I was knocked sideways by Tattoo-arm landing on his face beside me. He crawled onto his knees, retched and was sick and then went down again as someone else fell on top of him and a voice from the dark above me said," Come on then, lass. Up you get."

It was a grown-up voice. The sort that you automatically do what they say without arguing. You get some teachers like that. But by this I was crying and shaking so much I didn't care what anyone did to me, and I don't really remember even getting into his car, except that after a spell I was warmer and my legs were stinging where they had hit the stones. It was only then I realised it was the bloke who'd offered the lift earlier.

He didn't say anything to begin with, just U-turned in the middle of the road and headed back to town. After a bit though, he said, "You want to go to the police?"

That was the last thing I needed: answering questions and being stared at like I asked for it. "No. Thank you."

"How'd a cup of coffee go then, while you make your mind up what you want to do next?"

He pulled up outside a hotel.

"See that door?" – he pointed up the steps – "Inside to the right there's a ladies'. You go and get yourself cleaned up, eh? This your bag I fished out of the ditch? Right, then. Here, hang on a tick," he reached over into the back seat. "You'll die of cold like that. Have a lend of this until you warm up. It's too big, but it's respectable. "He handed me something soft and woolly. "When you're right, I'll be in the room opposite. Okay? See you then."

Jeez, but I was a mess. When I looked in the mirror, I was all mud and tears and hair. There was blood on my face too, but it didn't seem to be mine. My hands were still trembling too much to do anything with make-up, so I made do with splashing soap and water on my face and played with my hair until it looked half-way reasonable. The jumper was just great, but. It came right down to my knees, but it was so soft and a nice greeny colour and it smelled of aftershave.

For a second I thought, what if I nipped off now and left him waiting for me? But I was too tired to bother with tricks like that, and besides, where would I go? So I strolled out the ladies', making out I didn't give a fig if I stayed or not, and into the room the other side of the passage.

It was an old-fashioned pub, small and cosy with those high ceilings you get in old places, and there were real flowers, not plastic, on the tables. My guy was sitting by the fire, and that was real too. He was talking to this fat man the other side of the bar. He stood up when I came in and pulled out a chair. Get this, I thought, Mum would say "a real chauvinist smoothy". I felt bad, though, thinking of her just then.

He was older than I'd thought at first. Pretty ancient in fact, at least forty. But he looked clean and expensive. I mean he was only wearing jeans and a windcheater, but you could tell they didn't come from Target.

The barman came over with a mug of hot chocolate something – Milo or one of those drinks I hadn't had since I was a bub. I sipped the top. It was too sweet but I wasn't complaining. It was just that my hands were all wobbly still and shook when I tried to pick up the mug.

"Hey, hey, take it easy. It's all over now."

What I really wanted to do was cry, and my eyes were watering like mad, but I didn't want to in front of him, so I pretended the drink was too hot and made a joke of it. I ached everywhere, and I was so wrecked that if I'd have put my head on the table, I would have passed out there and then.

"Still want to go to Sydney?"

I wriggled my shoulders. I didn't want to go anywhere. "Okay" he said. "I don't mind seeing you right for Sydney, if that's what you want. On the other hand, I'm going to Melbourne and I'd be happy to take you along. Up to you."

It was all too much. I could see Mum. I could see her pacing up and down, hair flying everywhere, smoking one cigarette after another, like she does, and her lips would be pressed in and she'd be mad as hell – would she ever be mad! But I could see that long, quiet road and that would be pitch black by now. I couldn't help it. I put my head in my hands and howled and howled.

He was good. He didn't do any of that dumb stuff with handkerchiefs like they do in the movies. He didn't do anything. He waited until he could get a word in sideways and said, "Melbourne it is, then."

I'd catch some sleep in the car, I reckoned, it was so warm and comfortable. But I found I wasn't so sleepy after all, and because he didn't say much but did sort of listen, I got to talking to fill in the silence. And it all came out: Mr Brannigan, and Sharon and Dave and everything. And Mum. I was beginning to get seriously wound up about her.

"Oh gee, is she going to be wild."

"You want me to stick around and explain then?"

"Not unless you want to cop the flak too. She can be pretty mean when she's roused. Come back after and give me a decent burial, if you like."

That had him laughing and he reckoned he'd play it by ear.

When we reached our block I gave back the green jumper. The lift wasn't working as usual, and Ant Papadopolous and his gang were lounging in the stairwell, kicking each other and spitting – tough guys I don't think! They let us through but shouted and called once we were safely away. We had five floors to climb and you could hear that bloody Thompson kid screaming its lungs out all the way up.

I made out I was only make-believe scared. You know, cracking jokes and that. But I was honestly desperate inside. I just didn't know what was going to hit when I rang that doorbell. I sure didn't expect her to come flying out like she did, like a pink-padded missile, all hair and this daggy quilted dressing gown she'd grabbed from an Op-shop half a century ago. She nearly knocked me down, crying, "Vicky, oh my baby, oh Vicky", and hugging and kissing me. So next I'm bawling too, and hugging her because I didn't want to leave her really and I'd never noticed that I'm taller than she is now and how bony she was under all that pink padding, and honestly she's all I've got and I'm all she's got, and by the time we'd stopped entertaining the neighbours on our floor and the next, the man had gone. Faded into the night, him and his car.

"What man?" said Mum. "I never saw any man."

I went back to school the next day with a note saying I'd had a cold and found that Shaz and Dave had split up and he was eyeing off this slag in Year Seven. Old Brannigan gave me B+ for an essay and might have smiled but it'd have cracked his face. And Mum made a lasagne for tea.

And my knight in a shining Beemer? Did we ever see him again? Did he come back, marry Mum, sweep us off our feet?

Get real!

Only occasionally I get a whiff of expensive aftershave in a crowd and I find myself looking around, but I never see him. I never saw him again.

And times like when we've spent three hours clearing the block in the drain again and the water's running at last and Mum says, "See Vick. Men, who needs 'em?" And maybe she's right.

Still, when it gets really bad, I'd like to believe he's still out there somewhere.

STOCK PART NO.

By James Vanselow

When the sun goes down in Bakersville, Nevada, the trucks come out.

The leading 18-wheeler swings into Main Street. Briefly, the afterglow of the desert sun flashes off the aluminium truck siding, sending a wash of gold flooding through the front windows of Henry's General Store.

Henry Ackerman pauses in wiping the desert dust from the glass counter top and raises his head to fix his eyes on the trucks as they pass, counting each one.

"Five today, Marge, one more than yesterday."

"Pity they didn't stop and buy something," Marge replies, tugging at the frayed bottoms of her faded denim shorts, "we could do with their trade."

"You'd think they'd find themselves out of cigarettes once in a while, wouldn't you? What I can't figure out is why they come through here anyway, us not being on the highway anymore."

"That bypass road has sure cut our trade. No one on Route 59 would even know Bakersville existed if it wasn't for the sign at the turn-off."

Henry doesn't reply. Route 59 had been straightened some three years earlier when a bridge over a dry creek bed had been constructed. Now Main Street is used only by the ranchers and the few travellers bored enough with the monotony of Route 59 to wonder if a small desert town is anything like what they see in the movies. Bakersville never disappoints them. The dozen or so shop fronts of paint-flaking grey clapboard buildings baking under the desert sun contain the anticipated café with Laminex-topped tables and counter, and a petrol pump in front of a double-door building on which a sign in rusting metal advises "Mechanical Repairs". Apart from the Produce Store selling stockfeed and agricultural goods, Henry's General Store is the only surviving business. The shop windows of the other buildings have been painted over, to afford privacy to those that are now occupied as homes, and to lessen the prospect of vandalism to those which are not.

Henry edges out from behind the counter and makes his way out the front door onto the veranda. Standing there, his eyes narrowed against the sun's last glare, he watches as the trucks swing back onto the highway, and then goes inside.

"I called the County Sheriff's office two days ago," Henry says as he sits at the kitchen table drinking Coke from the shop's drink machine. "Couldn't tell me anything about the trucks. Said he had already had a call from Johnson at the garage, so he took a run out to check if the highway surface was okay. Nothing wrong with it that he could see, he said."

Henry raises the can to his lips and swallows.

"The deputy told me Johnson tried to get some plate numbers, but they were covered in dust. The most he could make out was something on the side of one of the cabs about recycling."

"God knows what anyone could recycle around here," Marge says and rises from her chair to turn the sink faucet on. "Rusted water pipes perhaps."

Henry says nothing, taking another mouthful of Coke. The water pipes can stay as they are, he thinks. He and Marge may not be in Bakersville much longer if trade doesn't pick up.

That night, Henry lies in bed thinking about the store, the town, the people that used to live here, the few ranchers who they now depend on for a living, how the town used to be when he married Marge only a few years ago. Young hopefuls, young and stupid he thinks. And the trucks. The trucks seem to be the only new thing to happen. Everything else exists in the past. Only the trucks can add life to the town, but they do not stop. Johnson, he thinks, and then falls asleep.

The desert sun slants low through the bedroom window. Henry feels the warmth and wakes, turning his head to look at the sleeping Marge before he rolls out of bed. He pulls on his jeans, check shirt and pushes his feet into sneakers. He steps into the bathroom and looks at his face in the mirror, notes the premature wrinkles around his eyes, draws a hand across his jaw, and decides not to shave. He goes out through the screen door of the room at the back of the store and makes his way along the sideway to Main Street. No trucks. Not that he expects any so early. Always at sundown, he thinks. He heads towards the garage, Johnson's garage.

"You there, Johnno?" Henry calls into the double doors, doors not shut for years.

"Yeah, course I'm here, I'm trying to get this wheel fixed before heat sets in, the bloody heat, always bloody hot here in the day."

"Keep working, don't let me stop you, I'll just talk away."

Johnson rolls a wheel from where it has been leaning against his workbench.

"Just came by to talk about the trucks. The deputy tells me you asked about them, same as me. Curious ain't it, the way they go by, same time, same direction, never come back, but always there again the next day at sundown."

"Yeah, funny they come here at all, never buy petrol or nothing from me."

Johnson lets the wheel drop, straightens up and pulls a pack of Lucky Strikes from the side pocket of his overalls. He jabs the cigarette between his lips and lights it, one hand shielding the lighter flame from the hot desert wind that has arrived in short gusts, stirring up the red dust. Johnson's fingers are cracked across the back, his palms callused. God, another few years here in this desert and I could look like that, Henry thinks. Not much more than forty, Johnno is, Rough hands, wispy hair, will Marge love me when I look like that? What will Marge look like, dried up by the desert?

"What d'ya want, anyway?"

"Just thinking. The deputy doesn't seem interested any more. How about we find out about the trucks ourselves. You know, follow them, see where they go."

"What's in it for us?"

"Nothing. Nothing except you'll find out what you wanted the deputy to tell you."

"That dumb-ass. Only phoned him up to get him running round about nothing."

Henry moves to the side of Johnson, out of line of the stream of cigarette smoke Johnson exhales.

Johnson's eyes recede deeper into their surrounding bed of wrinkles as he narrows them, looking down at the red dust on his boots. "Could give it a go. Make that deputy look bloody stupid if we find out something he should've known about."

Henry smiles. "I'll come around right on seven in the Bronco. We'll back up into your garage and wait for the trucks to come by. They won't be hard to follow. I'll tell Marge we're going to play cards for a couple of hours. I don't want her to think the desert sun has got to me."

"Perhaps Marge is only a woman, but she's going to think you're pretty bloody stupid driving your Bronco no further than you can spit."

"You're right. I'll tell her I am taking it to you to look at the tuning and we'll be playing cards after."

The sun is melting into the horizon when the first of four trucks wheels into Bakersville, swings around the corner into Main Street and heads south until once again entering Route 59. The driver of Truck 4 looks in his rear-vision mirror, carefully watching the vehicle some 200 yards behind.

"I reckon we've hooked one this time, Red," he says to his partner alongside him in the cab. "Ford Bronco, ya see it?" His partner, a thickset man who might not feel intimidated by anyone smaller than Hulk Hogan, nods and fixes his eyes on his side mirror.

"Two. He has a passenger."

"Okay. I'll signal Truck 3 to let them know we've got one hooked and using Plan B," the driver says. "Knowing the sort of people who drive Broncos, we may just need some help to reel this one in." The driver, a smaller baldheaded man with a goatee beard, flicks the headlights from high- to low-beam four times. Truck 3 immediately responds with its right indicator lights as it slows and edges half off the blacktop. Truck 4 gives a blast on its klaxon horn as it breezes past with the Bronco in tow.

"One of them's stopping, Johnno. They may be on to us. What do you reckon we should do?" Johnson removes the neck of a bottle of Jack Daniels from his mouth, drags the back of a hand across his lips and eases further down in his seat.

"Nervous Nelly, aren't you? They've probably blown a tyre. Just keep after the one we've been following. Hang back a bit and we can get away any time we like."

155

The Bronco keeps its distance from Truck 4 as the sun rims the horizon with its last rays and black velvet soaks up red desert dust.

"Shit. It's turning off. Can you see the other trucks?"

Johnson opens his eyes. "Nah, they must be ahead of him."

The Bronco throws up loose gravel as the twin beams of its headlights are extinguished by Truck 4's dust trail.

Four hundred yards off the blacktop, Truck 4 brakes, slewing to a stop across the narrow road.

"Bloody hell! Back up, back up!" Johnno yells. "They're on to us." Before Henry can select reverse, he feels the thump as Truck 3 noses in to close the net.

"Truck 4 to Bay 6," the loudspeaker booms. The driver of Truck 4 swings around outside the galvanized-iron-clad warehouse, and reverses into a concrete loading bay. A roller door opens, chain rattling. Six men emerge, two in coveralls, four in white coats. The rear doors of the truck are swung open, ramps pushed across the gap. Under the glare of arc lamps, the Bronco is reversed out onto the loading dock. The four men in white wheel two trolleys into the truck and, in a matter of minutes, emerge with a body on each.

A man in a black suit materialises from the surrounding darkness and takes a cursory glance at Henry's prone form, then moves to Johnson's. He rolls back Johnson's lips, sniffs his breath, lifts his hands, looks at his fingers. "Smoker and drinker. No profit in him." He turns to the men in white, "Give him another injection and drop him in the dumpster." He looks at the comatose Henry again. "This one seems sound enough. Take him over to Triage for assessment." The black suit blends into the shadows.

Black suit sits in a leather chair facing an older, white-haired man sitting behind a polished mahogany desk. "We did well tonight, boss. A catch of six vehicles and ten bodies for recycling. Actually, we got eleven, but one's an alcoholic and smoker. Lungs and liver probably shot, and kidneys not worth assessing."

The white-haired man nods, pressing the tips of his fingers together. "Good, good. We can't be too careful. We charge our customers top money and they expect the best merchandise. Kidneys are bringing $50,000 in Turkey now, livers double that, and hearts and lungs are topping $200,000 in Japan."

When the sun comes up sixty miles south of Bakersville, Nevada, the Parts Delivery vans roll out through the gates of Total Recycling Incorporated. The fertiliser trucks leave a little later.